# CLEAR SKIES IN THE DELTA

# CLEAR SKIES IN THE DELTA

TRACY LYNN SANDIFER-HUNTER

Palmetto Publishing Group
Charleston, SC

*Clear Skies in the Delta*



First Edition

Printed in the United States

ISBN-13: 978-1-64111-304-5
ISBN-10: 1-64111-304-9

*This book is dedicated to my Dearest Mother and Grandmothers who came before her, my dearest daughters, Erica, and Johnnay, Palmetto Publishers as well as all the people who love, dance, and sing in the golden sunshine. When we sat in the evening sun eating ripe red watermelon, just letting the sweet juice trickle down our feet, we didn't know that we were creating sunshine. When we inhaled the sweet aroma of Sunday dinner that our grannies labored over in the cool of the morning, mixing just the right amount of this and that, we didn't know that they were creating sunshine. When we inhaled the intoxicating rains that flowed down from the hills, mixed with that good-smelling country dirt, that was pure, golden, liquid sunshine. When we held our newborn babies tight in our arms, they told us that our generation would carry on, they would live and breathe in that bright sunshine, building, prospering, creating a world made from lessons learned of those who labored in the sunshine, making poetry out of pain. So I say unto you, live in that ever-glowing sunshine underneath the clear skies, and your soul shall be at rest..*

# FOREWORD

Oh, dear love, how the clear skies are blue for you, way far beyond the overcast. The yellow sun in the sky shall forever bask in your grace. You are a teacher. You are a giver. You are a mother. You are the fertile soil that grows the soul in this town. You are a blooming flower under an overcast sky. You are the sunshine of the Delta—my southern belle, the creator of all earthly creators. Our God sent me to you through your womb, and through your gifts. Something illustrious has been ignited. We boldly share our heritage with those who seek the Delta, changing hearts along the way. You are a a true Delta woman, walking around with no shoes, painting the overcast Delta sky with oils and words. The bubbling of buttered grits in a pot, sizzling breakfast pork sausage in a pan next to it, a skillet full of eggs whirling in a bowl on artificial marble counters; that is what every Saturday of my life is like whenever I'm with you. If water is nourishing, then you are water. You've taken your waterspout and watered an entire community, and that, my dear, is a God dream. You are a flower blowing in the Delta wind, steady and strong, waiting for the sun to come out again, patient and delicate under the watch of clear, blue overcast skies.

Your dear daughter,
Erica

CHAPTER 1

# EXODUS

Growing up in Mississippi, I was always fascinated with the tales my Mother Neeyla Jean told me about her life on the Money Road and how we ended up in Greenwood. As I listened to Neeyla's stories, time itself seemed to evanescence back into the shadows of her distant past. The words and memories erupt like ancient melodies on an old phonograph record player ever resounding from my childhood as my mind's eye travels to her accounts of where it all began. She recalled how the sky turned blacker than black in the middle of the day.

"Pitch black darkness gave way to daybreak, and the town sat in quiet whispers as it dutifully wrapped itself in the monotony of routine. Men with broad smiles and smudged lipstick on their faces emerged from their shanties in plaid shirts and stretched their denim and heavy work boots across long rows of white cotton fields to earn the meager wages of the day.

"Hey, baby, you left your lunch!" Big Momma yelled out the window to her husband. He quickly redoubled his steps back on up the street and retrieved his lunch pail from Big Momma's waiting hand. After giving her a loud kiss on the lips, he quickly made his way back up the road. Scattered tin cans from a neighboring yard tumbled in the wind. The sun sat squarely in its autumnal Southern sky, casting a luminous glare through the darkening black clouds. Hard winds whistled through the trees, while heavy rains tumbled like bricks from the sky. Without announcement, the sounds of freight trains could be heard in the distance. Neeyla recalled as she watched from an open window across the yard as the dark clouds loomed overhead.

She said that an F5 tornado had been predicted to hit the town of Money, which was causing my grandmother Carrie to pace the floors of the kitchen, contemplating the answer to the problem that now lay imminently before her, for to not take action would mean certain death for all of her six children as she stood in the middle of the kitchen floor with a look of horror and consternation on her face. The strong winds had pulled the entire wall from the back of the house. She didn't know what to do so she called on God. "Heavenly Father, please have mercy on me and my family. Lord please don't let us die in this storm," she loudly cried. Then without hesitation, and in a nervous fit of anxiety, she called all of her young children one by one, as the torrential storm would soon make its mark through the shanties of Money. "Neeyla, Archibald, Rufus, Luella, Eloise Oscar, Jabo, and Tracy! All ya'll come quick! The tornado is blowing the house away. This is it! Hurry! Bring yourselves here. Lord, please have mercy here! Ya'll get in here right now!"In an instant, we managed to run to her beckoning cries and pleas. Both wind and rain now heaved heavily against the walls of our home as destiny now lay at hand. Carrie had called us one by one, and we somehow had all gathered to pray that the hand of God would not only be with us, but would carry us through as the tornado swept through the small town of Money. Shuffling feet scurried hurridly and fell prostrate on the kitchen floor. The younger ones cried out in terror as they groped in the darkness clinging to my grandparents while Neeyla held me tightly in her arms. Hard rains poured through the wind-swept roof and beat against our backs. Gushing sounds of water permeated the interior of the shanty, and fear infused with quiet moans could be heard as Carrie and Jabo huddled over us praying out loud to perhaps shield us from the clutch of death as both the foundation and the seal of the house had begun to yield its contents.

The horror that ensued—the violence and deafening ferocity of the storm—seemed to spawn an eternity. However, suddenly all was quiet, and the tiny shack and its contents somehow had been swallowed in the abyss of time. The family sat in silence for a long time in bewilderment at the sheer horror itself because there was nothing left, but us and the kitchen floor that we had gathered on to pray. Although I was too young to remember it, Neeyla said that we all cried together and gave thanks to God that He had spared our lives. Then at once, as grass springs upward, the frantic yet motionless figures staggered about underneath steel gray clouds as one awakened from a horrific nightmare. As the news spread around the town, the people nervously searched through the debris and aftermath of the tornado to assess and salvage remains now lost in memory.

"I can't believe it," one of the men said, "that tornado came up from behind those woods sounding like a loud freight train running through here. I was headed to the fields with the rest of em, and all we could do was lie down in that big ole ditch down the road and hope and pray that the storm passed on by us. I aint never beem so scared in my life."

"You're right. Now we ain't got nothing left but a big ole living nightmare," another added.

"We sho is," they agreed. "God know what he be doing," added Uncle Sammy, we aint got nothing out here no way but sacks of cotton and sweat."

The storm had ended, but the familes were faced with the aftermath of suffering, as my family was now faced with even greater uncertainty and had no where to go. After hearing loud screams pour from our neighbor's house, Carrie told Neeyla, the oldest, to watch the younger five while she, Jabo, and the eldest son Archibald went to offer words of consolation and sorrow for their neighbor's children whose mother had perished in the storm.

"Neeyla, keep them children in the yard until we get back. Lord knows, the sorrow is bad enough."

Cries of anguish and loud screams emanated from the crowded three-room shack, for the inhabitants were mourning the loss of their beloved mother.

"I want Momma back!" cried the little ones between sobs and screams. "No, Momma's gone. She's gone! What we gonna do?"

The incessant cries of the three youngest children could be heard coming from the innermost parts of the flat. Jabo raised his arm in an almost hesitant stance and offered a quiet knock on the door.

"What do you want?" projected the voice on the other side.

"It's Jabo and Carrie from down the road, coming to check on you."

"Let me be; I don't want to talk to you." "Go away!"

Instead, they walked right on through. Carrie grabbed the distraught teen and held her close. "You know your Momma will be missed. We'll all miss her. You know you the oldest, Bess Anne. It's up to you, gal, to hold this family together. You hear me? God knows best, and He has the final answer. You just hold on, Bess Anne. God will see you through."

Neeyla, said, "My Dad's heart shone through like bright and shining liquid gold measuring the expanse of the sky. This was Daddy's heart the way she knew it to be when he wasn't drinking."

"I know, but it's not right with Momma gone. I am trying, but it's hard. How am I going to see after all these children by myself with no

Momma or Daddy? My question is why did this happen?" stated the young girl between bursts of soft cries.

"Come on." Carrie said as she held the crying teen tightly in her arms. "I'ma check on you first chance I get, and wanna see that pretty girl smile the next time I see you. I mean it."

In the meantime, two men engrossed in examining the exterior of the storm-torn shanties spoke in mournful tones.

Jabo explained, "I'll be back to help you rebuild this roof and the kitchen. We gon'e need to get all these kids to your folk's house before nightfall. Bess Anne is still a child herself, and your sister wouldn't have it any other way."

The two men stood motionless as silent giants, and for a long time dazed in a reverie of lost hopes and dreams buried in the wreckage beneath the storm. Words became silent tombs as the men motioned melancholy goodbyes as the moon waned warily and pitched itself against the quiet night sky.

Daybreak emerged, and the noise of the town's people erupted in muffled tones as they searched through the endless rubble and debris in search of what had once defined their lives.

Our family had spent the night with a neighboring family and was now waiting to ride the bus to Greenwood. In the meantime, we watched very pensively as our cousins and Uncle's wife outfitted themselves on the outskirts of the town to salvage their fragmented and broken belongings. Neeyla recalled, "Although I didn't realize it at the time, this would be our final farewell with the Money Road, and all of its gained hopes and lost dreams. I became engrossed in deep thoughts as I gazed quite contentedly at them for a long time while they tried to make some sense of what life had given them.

"Look what I found, Momma," said the child of four as she motioned toward the large, slightly aging mother. The mother, with a forlorn look of exasperation, mumbled in an almost inaudible voice, "What is that, girl?"

"It's Big Momma's blanket that she made. It's too heavy. Can you get it for me, Momma?"

The tired mother, in an instant, grabbed her small child into the folds of her large arms, and gently kissed the child on the top of her face. Suddenly she began pulling at the grimy quilt that her mother-in-law had pieced together many years from beneath the broken bottles and an upside down sofa. With the full brunt of her weight and a violent tug, she managed to rescue the torn quilt from the damp earth, shook the loose soil from it, and carefully examined it for lodging insects.

Meanwhile, the older children had managed to escape the scrutiny of the mother's keen eyes, and were engaged in a wild game of "it." The older boys were running in mad circles from the young son, who had a slight limp from a physical deformity.

"The last one to the step is a rotten egg!" the boys shouted. The children had made a home base of the sole remnant of a set of farmhouse doors and a lone set of storm washed concrete steps. The younger boy breathed heavily in and out as he attempted to catch his older brothers in a wild fit of anger. The mother angrily tossed her salvaged goods in the air. "Toby and Jessie Lee, , I've told you to stop chasing Little Sammy . You gon' upset his asthma. Don't you hear how he breathing? Now get yall's narrow-ass behinds over here and put all this here stuff in this basket before I lose my cool. Come here, Little Sammy. Boy, sit yo bad self down, for you get what they gon' get." Have ya'll seen Reena? Her fast tail ass ain't no where to be found on a day like this.

"Mama, it's hot out here," the older boy retorted as he obediently shuffled his feet in the direction of the basket.

"Well, boy, it's hotter than that in hell. Now Little Sammy, sit over there with your sister while me and your brothers put these things in the baskets."

Meanwhile, the scorching sun transformed into an opaque and translucent color as the mother and her children labored in the sun beneath sullen skies.

## CHAPTER 2

# EAST MCLAURIN

The trees stood silent in somber obedience to the swaying of the wind as we said our last goodbyes to the majestic Money Road. The road itself beckoned and called back memories of Big Mama's ghost and Mrs. Baker's ripe green tomatoes and sweet lemonade.

The trip to Greenwood was a monument of memories departing from what was, and what was to become, for we had created both home and heritage on the outskirts of Greenwood. Funny, I could still see them as if it were just yesterday, and Mrs. Baker had gone home to be with the Lord nearly two years now. Suddenly, I felt Mrs. Baker's gentle whisper and watchful presence standing over me, and I knew that Greenwood would be okay, for she had promised me that long ago summer that she would always be my special angel, watching over me and my baby, no matter where we went.

After Henry Baker married that razor-faced girl, he moved to Oxford, Mississippi, to study law. I guess I wouldn't be seeing much of his fine self after that. But then again, Henry would get that law degree and march his handsome hind right on back and rule with that same iron fist that his mom,Mrs. Clementine Baker had. She wasn't no politician, or anything like that, but money talks, and sho nuff walks. I didn't care about that, though. I just loved Mrs. Baker, and Lord knows I miss her so.

Greenwood itself was a maze of farming and agriculture that unraveled itself patiently before my widening eyes. Certainly, Neeyla was no stranger to the town. However, she had only seldomly ventured past the outskirts and the local downtown areas during her trips to town for the Bakers, and on occasions with Carrie. The neighborhoods on the other side of town resembled penny matchboxes stuck together with the windows cut out. The town itself evoked images of little elderly ladies peering from screened porches while children zoomed by on multicolored bicycles until the cricket cried its last cry. East Greenwood, which was between Highway 7 and Carrollton Avenue, reveled in a sea of lush clover grass and red clay dirt, and created a type of pastoral setting. The honeysuckle blossoms erupted from deep ditches above the smell of soybeans seeds from a neighboring plant, which had eroded to a massive heap of decay but sufficed for well-earned wages.

Because of our family's large size, we were subsequently temporarily divided among relatives and friends. The Red Cross and Salvation Army gave us hordes of clothing, gift certificates, and food vouchers. We couldn't have made it without their help. My mother and I, along with her two sisters, Eloise and Luella, ended up at the home of Mrs. Murtis Shack, a distant relative who was also from the foothills of Carrollton County. Murtis Shack was an aging, small-framed woman in her late fifties, who lived with her common-law husband Frank. Murtis wore her hair pulled back in a well-groomed coiffure to frame her slightly protruding, bubbly nose and lips, which gave her speech the effervescent sound of spit, cheek, and tongue.

The Shack's home itself was a screened-in box tightly fitted between neighboring shotguns, and in its encasing, mirrored the souls of its very inhabitants. The Shacks were icons of a fast-dying past with faded fedoras and Jackie O.-fitted empire waist dresses in Sunday colors of yellow and lime green; Frank's suits well resembled the forgotten look of yesteryear. Murtis was stylishly coquettish, and had had her share of men in waiting, but that season of her life was as faded as the heavy drapes that hung from the windows like monuments of time. Now, she would only have Frank's eyes of her far-fleeting passionate youth. Inside the shotgun stood the relishes of time; blurred photographs of her parents rested peacefully on the mantle over the hearth, and fragile, yellow-tinted crocheted doilies were carefully dispersed on the top of the mantle as if time itself would not dare move them.Murtis would often intone when she was thoroughly bored with Franks' company and not feeling like no hanky panky, "Frank, I got the headache." Both lust and love and mad midnight fiascos had sealed the deal more than twenty years ago. Now they would serve for each other's good company and talk their days into nights. Typically, Murtis would be up before sunrise preparing her famed sweet buttermilk biscuits as Frank's gazing eyes peered intently from behind his *Greenwood Commonwealth*. Frank spoke little, but took in much. The entire kitchen savored the smell of good, country, frying bacon and sausages as Murtis daintily doled them out on waiting plates.

"Good morning, Neeyla, Luella, and Tracy. Did you all sleep well last night? I hope Frank's snoring didn't disturb you much. I hardly slept a wink. Well, I hope you're in the mood for my famous sausage, bacon, and biscuits. Mama taught me how to make 'em from scratch when I was a very young girl, and I been making 'em ever since. In fact, it was my cooking, and my big booty that drove Frank crazy. Well, don't tell nobody, but we ain't really legally married. I wouldn't, on account of that Ole Belle. She might have come back, and Frank would have sent me on my way up the creek without a paddle."

Frank stared real hard at Murtis for a long time, and shoved the newspaper closer to his face.

As time progressed, we became accustomed to the daily routine and customs of the Shack family as they lived in the ritual of their daily lives, with breakfast and supper always served at the exact time, with no lunch for Murtis. She was always watching her figure, saying, "Don't no man want no fat woman." She recalled wild tales of her early twenties when she and Frank began courting, only to find out that Frank had been married twice previously, and now Murtis was his third common-law wife. She giggled as a young girl recalling their distant past.

"We all lived in Carroll County, and were all members of Faith Baptist Church when he was still married to his second wife Belle. Frank was on the deacon board, and was quite a handsome, stocky one. But that yellow gal he was married to couldn't concentrate on the preacher or the sermon for trying to watch Frank and her little boyfriend in the choir. She was comely, but wild to the core. Truth of the matter was, she was stepping out on Frank, and Frank was, well, trying to step out on her. However, I put my foot down. See, I was too decent and ladylike to be fooling around with a married man. No, sir, my mama told me that adultery was an awful bad sin. Yet I could hardly take up the Sunday school offering for Frank's gazing eye watching my backside. Girls, I was real fine and curvy in them days, but no, I didn't go out like that so Frank could only look but not touch. All the while, his eyes told me that he wanted me real bad. You see, the eyes never lie, but I wasn't about to play with him like that. As the old folks say, it will come out in the wash. To make a long story short, it wasn't long before Mrs. Thang got herself knocked up by choir boy. Well, everyone at church knew that they was liking each other, and then Little Frank junior came out deep dark-skinned just like his daddy, choir boy. All the while, his Momma Belle and Daddy Frank were both practically white looking. Frank must have been real hen-pecked, 'cause he was so proud of that baby, when he should have full well known that it wasn't his baby. The baby came out identical to his daddy Fred Foley, with skin, big ears, and all. Frank, all the while, blinded to the truth, saying that that baby took his grandmamma's color. Well, we all just sat back and passively watched until one day Ms. Thang didn't come home. Over a period of months, Frank fell into a deep depression, left with his two children to raise along his stepdaughter. We all were sure that Fred had killed her, since he had already been whipping on her, and she was foolin' Frank like she was falling down, only to find out that Fred went missing too. It almost killed Frank dead. Well, a few years later, it was discovered by some relatives that they had run off to Kansas City and tied the knot, leaving Frank with all three of them children to raise. Hell, I felt sorrow for him, and would go over on the weekends and help him out. After I knowed for sure that Ms. Thang wasn't coming back, I moved in with him and helped him raise all of those hard-headed-ass children, and finally they all left, with Bobby Frank going off to college at Valley State. He called me momma since I was the only momma he ever knew, and had raised him like I gave birth to him. He now lives in Tennessee with his own family now, and still calls me and comes to see about me, still bringing me gifts during the holidays. After that, I could finally be all Frank's, but by then we was too tired and too old to enjoy it. And Frank is way yonder older than me," declared Murtis. Frank scowled. "Murtis, why don't you mind your own damn business. Little Frank is over thirty, and Belle has been dead over ten years. Now let that woman rest. Besides, you and I have been married almost thirty years. Why you gotta always bring up something that happened a hundred years ago? Now, I'm sure Neeyla and her sister have better things to do than listen to your old wives tales."

"Mr. Frank, I don't mind," said Neeyla. I really wanted to ask her what had actually happened to Bobby Frank's mom, Belle, but decided not to make matters worse. Therefore, I would ask when we were all alone out of Frank's presence. Neeyla would vividly recall to me how she giggled deep down on the inside knowing all the time that she and her sisters, Luella and Eloise, would laugh all night in the dark of their room at the Shacks and their daily antics. Now that my Mother Neeylawas approaching nineteen, she started assisting the Shacks in their daily chores and errands.

Before long, with the Shack's assistance, my family succeeded in securing a small two-bedroom home in the center of East McLaurin. The home was situated right down the road from the Black folk's cemetery, and would be our very first home in town. Rumor had it, that after nightfall, the ghosts would freely roam from house to house. I guess Big Momma's ghosts from the Money Road rode right on with us to Greenwood, and had now sided with the ghost of East Barrentine, as one night I saw an ominous figure looming from the wall and menacing my presence. When Momma, Neeyla Jean, questioned what this figure looked like, I told her that it resembled the shape of my uncle's gun rack, and had on a big boxing glove. From that moment on as long as I could remember, my Aunt Eloise and Oscar would terrorize me with taunts of this horrific apparition, the Black Hand Man that I had seen as a four-year-old child so many years ago.

Eloise, Oscar, and I were the younger ones, and would often amuse ourselves in the afternoon playing in the rich, thickly carpeted clover grass, playing for hours on end, making flimsy necklaces and playing make believe we were on a faraway enchanted island. I can still smell the aroma of deep purple blackberries that grew in glorious patches from that rich black and red clay soil as Grandma's Tide-washed laundry blew in the wind. When chance happened, we would sometimes find mounds of these succulent berries behind forgotten tree stumps in hidden places behind the house, and would relish their succulent sweetness in spite of being warned about snake berries. Grandma Carrie said that if she caught us eating them she would beat the hell out all of us, but we paid no mind to that, though. We just kept right on eating and sucking the juice out of them.

CHAPTER 3

# DOWNTOWN GREENWOOD

During that time, Greenwood seemed to exude a more ethereal pastoral landscape than of lately. Springtime was anew, and had put on it splendid color of blushing pinks and dewy whites

Around my fourth birthday, Neeyla Jean told me that we were going downtown so that she could find a job since she was close to twenty. Neeyla brushed my long kinky ponytails until they resembled the texture of soft cotton, tamed them with two baby blue barrettes, and dressed me in a soft lavender toddler's dress with a matching belt. Neeyla, who had the mature look of a beautiful twenty year old, knew just what she wanted in life, wore a fitted pantsuit with matching platform heels Neeyla had very expensive tastes and said that cheap clothes tear up when you wash them. Neeyla's skin's was the color of brown sugar and she favored her Grandmother Lula Belle with stoic Choctow features, thick black hair, and a well built frame that made the men take a second look. On top of being real fine and curvy, my Momma was real smart too. She wrote a song called "Homestead" that won her a contract with Sony Records in California, but she couldn't afford the recording fee. We strode quickly past the cemetery, past the old teacher's homes, and past the Broad Street Park, walking at a steady pace with my mother's clinched hand pulling me alongside her.

As we got near the edge of our neighborhood, my quick and curious eyes spotted a field of bright yellow daisies bursting forth in their perfumed delight as they danced carelessly in the breeze. My childhood instincts and love of nature beckoned me to a wild run toward the beautiful wildflowers, but Momma's tight grip spoke in an inaudible tone, with "Don't you dare think that you are going to touch them dang wildflowers. Do you want your little behind spanked? All it's going to do is aggravate your eczema." However, I smudged my nose and played it safe knowing that there would be plenty times to delight myself in the wonderful flowers that grew plentifully at the edge of the field in our own yard. For now, I would continue to play it off and amuse myself at the flowers from afar.

Neeyla's love was both protective and ruled by ferocity, which sometimes presented itself in a calypso of cursing; therefore, I understood well enough to know not to test the waters. The town's streets were bustling with 1972 Monte Carlos and Thunderbirds occupied with smiling and eager occupants, who quickly drove past out short strides. However, one convertible Monte Carlo redoubled and slowly followed behind.

The driver rolled down the window, saying behind dark shades, "Umm, umm, hey, pretty momma, you and that little one don't need no ride, do you?"

Neeyla offhandedly remarked, "Hay is for horses, and did I ask your ass for a ride?"

"Mmm, mmm, I like 'em feisty."

Neeyla clutched my hand tighter and proceeded to walk faster until he just backed back and drove out of sight. By this time, we had nearly reached the outskirts of our own neighborhood, and were situated directly across WC Williams School. Neelya told me that she wanted me to attend there once I was old enough. As we quickly walked past the school, Carrollton Avenue was directly in the center of town, stretched out on two ends by Chinese grocery stores, Sunlight and Acme, Ace's Hardware, Ray's Bait Shoppe, and Glover Mane's Hair Grow Products. My grandmother relished and infused our home on Saturday mornings with the eye piercing smells of sulphur and pressing comb, which lingered around the house for weeks like left over company that refuses to leave.

Downtown Howard Street was a whir of more brightly colored cars racing amidst a broad expanse of hardware, clothing, and household item shops.

"Momma, can I have a donut?" I inquired as we made our way to the edge of Shirley's Donuts and Goodman's Shoe Store.

"Not now," Neeyla remarked. "Wait until we get ready to go home."

We kept walking past the busy shops as I noticed graceful white women with well-manicured hands, graceful haircuts, and dainty dresses as they stole past us with an air of imperviousness. I thought these women were real-life versions of the beautiful Barbie dolls that my Aunt Reena, who lived in Chicago, bought for me during Christmas time. Reena was actually our cousin, but ever since I was little, she'd told me to call her Aunt Reena.

As we entered a store that said Five and Ten Cent Store on the outside, a tall man with mixed grays and brown hair greeted us with a great big, "Hello, what can I help you with?"Neeyla told him that she needed some screws to fix the hinges on a record player. He quickly motioned her in the direction of the hardware, while I fancied myself in a haven of yellow ducks floating in a pond of water. The store owner looked at me smiled, and asked if I wanted to pick up one of the little ducks. He explained it to me that it was a game, and if I picked up the right duck, I would win a prize. Afterwards, I smiled in amazement as I focused in on the best duck, and after some thought, picked up a duck, which floated right in front of me.

He then said, "Look at you, smart pretty girl."

He then handed me a tiny doll, which was wrapped tightly in plastic. I very politely said thank you as I giggled with sheer delight.

"Ma'am, what's your name?" inquired the shop keeper.

"Neeyla Jean. And this here is my only baby, Tracy Lynn. You might know my father Robert Sandifer, and his brother Willie. They do a lot of plumbing in these parts."

"Well, wouldn't you know?" He smiled. "You Jabo's daughter? I had him and his brother to do some plumbing for my shop, and never would have guessed it. By the way,you sure are a big fine looking country gal.Neeyla paid him seventy-five cents for the screws for the record player, along with some cookie cutters for baking which I still own to this day. She quickly walked out of the store and rolled her eyes at him without saying another word.

"Do come again, and bring Tracy with you so she can play the duck game," he yelled out. She simply grabbed my hand and started walking faster.

My fondest memories of my early life in downtown Greenwood ebb and flow like tidal waves coming back up to a distant shore filled with memories and going to the Five and Ten Cent Store with all of it curiosities.

Monday morning came, and all in the house was quiet except Carrie's intermittent clanging of pots and pans in the kitchen. She had just come back in the house from hanging the day's wash on the clothesline that spanned nearly the entire length of the middle of the backyard. Neelya had secured a job at Rocky Manufacturing Company; Oscar, Eloise, and the older teens were in grade school. Davis Ray, who was Granny's youngest son, was nearly a year old, and was fast asleep in his crib.

As she put away the morning's dishes and sat at the kitchen table to quietly sip from her mid-morning's coffee cup, I decided to ask, "Grandma, can I have some of your coffee?"

"Coffee makes your head hard, and besides, it's for grown folks. However, if you will go in the living room and bring Grandma the dust pan, she might save you a few sips."

I gleefully hopscotched through the kitchen, trying not to wake my uncle, because he was sure to end my quiet time with Grandma Carrie as I savored her rich, golden-colored coffee she sweetened with condensed Pet milk.

Evening would find itself each day with the usual noise and mirth in the house with the older children home from school, and Neeyla home from work. Jabo would wrestle and horseplay with us until he would fall fast asleep after a long day of plumbing. Once the older ones were home, Davis Ray and I were allowed to go outside with the rest of them to join in on games of jump rope, hopscotch, and cat's cradle. We played these games of childhood, soaking up the evening's sun until Carrie's fried chicken and gravy sent smoke smells that it was time to go in and eat.

CHAPTER 4

# CARROLLTON AVENUE

Carrollton Avenue is forever etched in my memory as one long pathway, which connects Greenwood in its intricate maze to all the other neighborhoods.

The incessant crowd poured in and out of Johnson's Street Fish Market like bees to honey to savor the smell of the freshly fried catfish, pan trout, and buffalo fish as it hovered over the neighborhood, intoxicating our senses with smells of the South. After moving off East McLaurin, Carrie moved her family into a large white farmhouse on Carrollton Avenue that had been converted to an apartment. My family lived in the centermost part of the farmhouse, and Baby Seal, a lively inquisitive neighbor who lived in the first apartment on the outside, occupied her time spying out of her window, or listening behind glass bottles to the merriment of the Sandifers. Although we never knew Baby Seal's real name, Neelya would teasingly call her "Baby Seal" because she would slick in and out of her front door as a seal slicks in and out of water.

Buddy, our white neighbor, lived behind us with his huge German Shepard named Cindy. I was sure that Buddy was going to let Cindy break loose from that leash and kill every nigger in our house. Neeyla told me that Cindy had been trained to hate Blacks. Now I always wondered how this was, and made it a point never to get too close to Buddy's fence, or go near Cindy. On the other hand, my Aunt Eloise, who was always business-like, found out that Buddy loaned payday loans to people, marched right on back there, and asked for a loan. When Grandma Carrie found out about this, she wanted to slap the living daylights out of her for going back in the first place, but didn't, because she needed one too.

The apartment itself was led in by a long corridor that contained a large hall mirror that Carrie eventually accidentally broke while hurling a brick at the older children Neeyla and Rufus, who had decided to test the waters and try out their young adulthood. The brick sent the glass crashing into a thousand smithereens as the teenagers hauled butt moving out of the way. In the heart of the home, there was a large living room with a full bathroom to the right upon entering. Carrie's bedroom was the first bedroom on the left. Neeyla, Luella, Eloise, and I slept in the same room, the middle bedroom, and Archibald, Rufus, Oscar, and Davis, slept in the last bedroom. After Archibald married his true love from Mississippi Valley State University, and left home for good, Rufus designed the room in matching shades of funky red. Carrie would often make her nighttime rounds with feet in shuffle through our room late at night to make sure Rufus and Oscar were in bed, and not sneaking cigarettes, but that was night.

Saturday morning after breakfast, the kitchen led one right through the backdoor, leaving a straight trail for mad see-saw games and chasing down butterflies, and lightning bulbs until there was very little life left in them. However, we would spend most of our after school and summer afternoons making lively mud cakes from the rich, red clay dirt, and playing hopscotch on the perpendicular walk with large brightly colored sidewalk chalk. Afterwards, we would pass time claiming what we imagined would be our future.

"That my car!" I shouted as a shiny new silver Buick with matching silver rims sped past us.

We would intermittently play this game for hours on end, trying to outdo each other between games of tag and hopscotch. Before the game's end, heavy cumulous clouds started forming beyond the horizon, and suddenly big droplets of heavy teardrops began falling from the sky as Davis and I made a mad dash for the front door. Inside were the hushed sounds coming in with the rain. By now the rain was coming down in flatbeds of white sheets while dancing a frigid dance upon the roof. Once the storm began, we were never allowed to make any sounds, or do anything that required anything outside of breathing, since our family had survived the tornado in Mississippi. Carrie wanted all of us to get in the closet, but we couldn't, since there were only two closets and too many of us to fit in either of them. On top of that, we couldn't even rattle a piece of paper while God was doing His work. I really couldn't understand it then, but as I grew older, I understood that my granny literally saw her home blow away before her very eyes with only her family left on the kitchen floor. I would imagine that I would have made my chaps shut up and be quiet too after witnessing all of that.

So we all just sat there in the dark as the rain came down late in the afternoon to wash the dirt and footprints of the deceased off the earth. Evening gave way to night, and after we had all eaten, Carrie decided to sit back in her comfy big chair to hand sew some new red gingham kitchen curtains. She said, "Flipadiddy, I am going to show you how to thread a needle and sew on your hand using a thimble."

I was around seven years old at that time, and was now ready to show off my artistic prowess of sewing by hand. I had been drawing since I was five, and now I would learn to sew. This would be the first of many Saturday evening sewing projects that I looked forward to and relished as we would labor upon hour's end, chasing the fabric with the tip of the tiny pointed needle.

After tentatively watching Carrie knot the end of the thread and create the familiar railroad stiches on the outstretched fabric, she then instructed me to sew across the entire length of the fabric. After she was done showing me how to tie a knot on a finished seam, she said, "I want you to sew these pieces together so that you can practice your straight stiches while I work on creating an embroidered flower for the top of the valance."

"Grandma, did I get it right?" I inquired as I very intuitively sewed the bright red gingham together.

She said, "That will do, but you must practice often to perfect it, except on Sunday, because that is the Lord's Day, and you must keep it holy. As with anything, Flipadiddy, you must be patient to reap the rewards of your labor."

I never forgot those lessons given to by my grandmother so long ago as a child, for she was of the generation who took back from injustice, whipped it into submission, and then put it to the side to carve out freedom for her family.

By this time, Carrie and Jabo had long ago grown tired of fighting each other, and had called it quits after over twenty years of a loving but tumultuous marriage. Consequently, Jab had sided with a wig-wearing woman named Faye who was equally as alcoholic. Neeyla said he had met his soul mate, and that they would be together until death did them part. In the cool of the evening, we would often sit on the green porch chairs in front of the house and wait for the sun to go down. Then, out of nowhere, we would spot them a mile off, Jabo and Faye, dancing a rhythmic drunken dance, a type of running drunk all the way down the sidewalk. As they got nearer, you could smell the sweaty mixture of intoxicants mingled with body odor.

They were like a sci-fi modern day Hansel and Gretel. Faye was a very thin woman in her forties, with deep depression lines in her face from years of drinking and neglect. She had a strong fascination for my long black braids that lay abundantly across my back, and would always lovingly rub them until Neeyla snatched her hand back, saying under her breath, "Keep your drunk ass hands out of my child's hair." Eloise and Luella told me that Faye didn't take baths, and that she would cause all of my hair to fall out just by touching it. I sort of liked her, though, and could tell that her smile was honest. Although often intoxicated to the point of delirium, my grandfather possessed a tight-lipped sincere smile that could melt a heart of gold beneath his floppy fisherman's cap. He would always reach down and hug me, and speak in slurred muffles, "Tracy Macy, how my little grandbaby been doing?"

Afterwards, he would always reach for Neeyla and attempt to give her a big ole drunk hug, but of course Neeyla, being Neeyla, would push him back with her fair share of profanities under her voice while mumbling to herself, "Get your drunk self off of me now.""Neeyla Jean, let me hold something, and ahhhh, Momma," he would say as he dogged her play licks.

Neeyla loved her dad true enough in her own way, but was just plain ole stubborn in her willingness to reciprocate what she felt should have been freely given on the Money Road. Of course, Grandpa would always give his favorite girl her share of drunken kisses. He really didn't care if Faye liked it or not. She would just stand there with both hands on her bony hips saying, "Jabo, you tryna quit me." By this time, Carrie was hanging over her lawn chair, crying laughing with the children. Faye then threw back her wig in disgust and stomped down the sidewalk yelling unknown profanities and declaring, “I don’t want you no mo’. Tryna play me for a fool. You know yoself Carrie is ugly. I’m fine, and she ain’t.”

Of course, the laughter would continue all evening, even when Faye and Jabo were well out of sight.

CHAPTER 5

# LOVE OF A LIFETIME

That night the shadows played solitaire against the quiet of darkness, and I covered my head as not to see the many faces of night and their ensuing terror.

The grownups had assembled themselves in the middle room and were speaking in hushed sibilant whispers.

"Jab and Faye need to stop all that drinking and carrying on," I heard them say. "Faye, she right shapely, but her face will kill a mule dead. Wonder where he got her from."

"Who knows? My guess is the places where they hang out. By the way, she has a day job working for a prominent doctor, both she and her sister. They say she's one heck of a cook. Working for who and what did it! Well, from the looks of her, I certainly can't tell. Well, rich white folks love their maid's cooking. Don't y'all know that!"

"Cut it out and go to bed. It's no time for judging," Carrie added. "The golden rule tells us to judge not that we be judged."

Whether one could call this cheating remains to be unknown, but Neeyla said Grandma's fast self was skinning and grinning, and courting a tall country freckle-faced man from Carroll County named Alvin White.

"They too old to be carryin' on like that out there in the dark of the night in his truck, kissing like some teenagers, and she even older than he is."

We didn't know exactly how she met him, or how it all started.

Neeyla one day, just out of the blue, said, "Where that man of yours at? You ain't fooling me, and I know why you going up to the hills every Sunday to see Grandma Lula Belle."

Carrie just stared at her for a long time until she silenced the sarcasm.

My mother Neeyla was every bit of Daddy Jabo's daughter, minus the drinking, but her mouth was an arsenal of cursing and insults with a ready supply handy. Well, we didn't have to wonder why Carrie left Jabo because somebody was bound to be killed. Sometimes we would adventure totip toe down the hall at night when we heard Alvin's loud truck pull up in the driveway. We stood there like silent giants for a long time trying to peer through the darkness.

"Aaaaahhh, hmmmm, hmmmmmm . . . "We could hear them hugging and carrying on like they were kids—a hot mess if we ever saw one. "Oooh wee! Carrie out there trying to make another baby!" I yelled.

Neeyla quickly slapped her hands over my mouth and said, "Shut your loud ass mouth, or go back where you came from."

Then we listened harder, and heard her say, "Stop, man, we can't be doing this out here. I have to get in the house before we wake up the neighborhood." When we couldn't see their shadows anymore, we figured they must have been getting it on in that truck.

Carrie wasn't trying real hard to get out of that truck because she was probably smiling all the while she was saying stop. Davis was her last baby she had when she was close to forty by her ex-boyfriend, and now was trying to add number eight to the clan. However, it was long before Eloise let on that we had been eavesdropping on them and staring out the window at night, so they decided to find a little rooming house on the other side of town, but Neeyla's friends told her about that too. Alvin himself was a very tall, fair-skinned man, with bright flashing eyes. He usually came to town with muddy work boots and heavily soiled farm clothes, which were rank to high heaven. Neeyla's smart mouth, as usual, would ask, "Why Alvin walk around with them muddy boots on? Don't he know better to come here like that?"

One day Carrie told us that he was coming to dinner with us and that we best act right."What in the hell?" remarked Rufus until we were all laughing, including Grandma.Neeyla offhandledly remarked, "I hope he takes a bath and does not bring that stankin' smell back into this house."

Carrie smirked and rallied back. "Neeyla, you should be ashamed of talking about that man like that, because he takes baths."

"In what a sewer?"

Now Luella and Eloise were adding their voices to the loud guffaw of laughter as Rufus joined in. Carrie then told all of her children to mind their own business, because she and Alvin were going to be together, and that was just all there was to it.

Eloise smarted out, "At least he can take a damn bath."

Before Eloise had barely got the words out of her mouth, Carrie reached way back into last year and brought a hot sailing lick smack dead on Eloise's sallow cheeks.

Oscar started laughing again, talking about, "Ooooh, wee! I heard that lick."

Eloise gritted her teeth and asked Oscar what in the hell he was staring at.

Carrie then yelled, "All ya'll bastards leave out of here and go to your rooms!"

Time erupted and emerged itself through summer rain and winter storms. In the midst of summer vacation, Grandma Carrie told Neeyla to wash and comb our hair since we would be going to Holcomb to visit Momma Lula Belle on Saturday, who was Carrie's mother and our great grandmother. That night, after a good head washing, Neeyla's heavy hands parted and snatched my coily locks till I screamed at the top of my lungs, "Ahhhhhhh, Momma! You hurtin' my head!"

"Girl, hush yo mouth, and this ain't hurtin' you," she would say, and kept right on combing and pulling the tangles out. Later, she pressed my thick tresses, and tightly plaited them back into two stiff braids. The entire house was filled with lanolin hair grease and straightening comb sulphuric smells. Folks used to burn hair on the stovetop back in them days, because they said if the birds built a nest with it, then all of the person's hair would fall out. Funny thing was, we had more superstition than we had money. We had to be especially careful with the mirrors in our house, because the ole saying was that if one broke a mirror, he or she was condemned to seven years of bad luck.

On the other hand, we hardly slept that night for the eagerness of riding through the country to Holcomb. Grandmother Lula Belle lived far in the country in Holcomb, Mississippi. The trip to the country took us through undiscovered turn roads and fields of high grass rising from ancestral tombs of Indian mounds buried high upon the earth's bosom. The grass tumbled and danced in merriment as we made our way through the winding backroads lost but not. Grandma Lula Belle's house set high upon a raised platform south of the Yalobusha River. The long, wide front porch seemed to welcome us with open arms. Somehow this land felt different. The land smelled of red clay country dirt that had been dug and molded with native hands and shaped by native blood into clay vessels. The voice of ancients could be heard in the whistling trees.

Lula Belle, who had heavy, broad hands, tight lips, and high Choctaw cheekbones mingled with African features, was the color of warm oatmeal.

Her dark eyes would often dart back and forth as she grinned her tight-lipped pert and flirtatious smile. She embodied a spirit of a life that reflected hardtoil and labor, as she lovingly looked on her family. Her house smelled of cleaning liniment, and hair pomades. After a warm-hearted welcome of overdue hugs and spitty kisses from our aunts and uncles, we were told to wash our hands and prepare to eat dinner. On the dining table next to the pot-bellied stove, there was always an abundance of savory field peas, and okra, turnip greens, and ham hocks, country ham, fried chicken, pans of country cornbread, buttery candied yams, and sweet banana pudding. With her bare hands, she had borrowed from the red clay land where our ancestors slept, and this was home.

Once, when all the adults had gathered in the front room and told all the children to go to the back and play, we sneaked in the hallway and listened to the grown folk's conversation. Great Grandma Lula Belle, who was born the granddaughter of freed slaves, had worked her entire life as a domestic. She later gave birth to a white baby that she had to give away. Neelya said that Grandma Lula Belle couldn't keep that baby on account of it looking mostly white. Although she wasn't allowed to raise that baby, her baby was given the best of everything, and sent off to a fine college. Only her daughter didn't stay there long. She fell in love with her college professor, and the last thing we heard was that she had gotten married and ran off to California. I guess he just couldn't keep his hands off that little pretty brown-eyed girl. He must have fallen in love too deep, because he just couldn't restrain himself.

Of course, these conversations were held in secret places, behind closed doors, and cut off from the children's listening ears, but we children had our ways of gaining access to them, and secretly carried them curiously in our hearts as frozen monuments in time.Meanwhile, I was growing taller and thin faced as days turned into nights, and so I preoccupied my time with being first grade. Davis and I had exhausted all possibilities of claiming the best car and sidewalk hopscotch. I had developed a passion for reading Grimm's fairy tales and recreating "Draw Me" contest drawings from the magazine. The characters themselves took the form of ancients from bygone eras. I readily engulfed myself in a maze of childhood fantasy and bewilderment as I poured over Rapunzel, Snow White and the Seven Dwarfs, and even Sleeping Beauty. Each tale, richly illustrated, beheld uncharted territories and unclaimed treasures. I labored over page after page for hours upon hours, and sometimes even imagined myself as a character in the tales. I would often draw the characters from the tales, and make clothes for them out of Grandmother's quilting scraps.

Late in the afternoon, my dad, James Roscoe, came home from Florida. He was driving a black Thunderbird and had on a little black fedora with shiny blackbird feathers in it. When he got out of the car, his smile was as wide as the ocean when I leaped into his arms.

"Ohh, Daddy's big baby is growing big."

"Daddy, I miss you."

"I miss you, too, sweetheart. Where's Momma?"

"She's in the house. I'll go get her." I ran in the house and yelled, "Momma! Daddy outside!"

Neeyla was standing on the front porch in two minutes flat, with a long house coat on and rollers in her hair. Neeyla had her hands on her hips and her mouth poised for whatever was about to erupt from it.

Dad looked at her and laughed real loud. "Girl, I always liked that fire in your blood. Now stick that lip back in, girl. You know I love you, with yo sexy self."

"Where yo woman at? We ain't heard from yo ass in forever. Don't come round here acting like you Daddy Dearest."

"Ahh, babes, why you gotta be so mean?"

By this time, my daddy had me in his arms, holding me tight. His beard was sticking my face; I could smell his cologne, and see the feathers on his hat blowing in the wind. This was my dad, and I felt safe.

"Roscoe, when you going to learn to think with your other head? All you doing is running around here making babies, and ain't halfway taking care of none of 'em. And you better not look like you want to kidnap my baby again and take her back to Florida. She ain't lost nothing in no hot assEverglades Florida."

"Don't worry, baby. I'm gon' get the girl something. I love this little angel more than life itself. This Daddy's baby."

"Roscoe, I hope you just heard what I said, and I ain't playing with yo ass either."

"Why if it ain't Roscoe! Let me hold something," said Grandma Carrie, walking out the screen door.

"Hey, Miss Carrie, my favorite queen!"

"Don't be trying to butter my momma up bastard because you heard what I said."

"Miss Carrie, I'm back here trying to show your daughter and my baby the world, but I just can't get through to her. Neeyla Jean, sunshine! Baby! You and my baby is going back with me," he said as he was reaching out to give Neeyla a big hug.

"Roscoe, don't touch me! You just make sure you have my child back here before dark," said Neeyla as she turned her back and went back in the house.

All the while Roscoe was smiling as I jumped quickly in the car. He drove off slowly, winking his eyes at Neeyla, who was still standing in the door rolling her eyes at him. My father and I had fun shopping that day, and later went to the circus. Since he didn't come to town much, I got used to it being just me and Neeyla.

School had let us out to bask in the suns of summer, and we would find ourselves sitting on the front steps in the cool of the day eating Alvin's ripe red watermelons as the sticky sweet seeds stuck to the tops of our bare feet. Grandma Carrie would sometimes scold us for eating watermelon seeds because she said that they made your stomach hurt. Yet this didn't faze us either, and like always, we just went right on eating sweet watermelon seeds not paying any mind to what she said.Carrie had cleaned everything spic and span, and the entire house smelled of Money House Blessing Spray. Folks used to spray their entire homes with it to bring blessings and ward off evil spirits. I think that purple can must have had a lot of power in it, the way folks used it. The older children spied on her and watched out the corner of their eyes with resentment as she poured Chantilly perfume over her lacy lavender blouse.

Eloise abruptly stated, "Any other time, she wouldn't be doing all this cleaning. I guess she trying to get stuffed up with another baby. It's just going to be in there whining, because I'm not seeing at it. I'm sure in the sam hill not. It's already enough heathens in this house, and Davis and that bird-faced Flipadiddy are more than a notion."

By this time, Neeyla was staring her down real hard in the face, so she didn't say another word.

That evening, Alvin came home for dinner, and we ate liver, rice, and gravy smothered in sweet Vidalia onions, turnip greens, golden-brown cornbread, sugary sweet iced tea, and homemade chocolate cake with deep fudge icing. He didn't wear the muddy boots, and had on clean clothes and heavy cologne, which only amplified the musky smells. All of the siblings were friendly and cordial, and waiting for the right moment to burst into wild outbursts of laughter on account of his peculiar yet friendly nature. However, Neeyla was waiting for the moment for the boat to be rocked, and indeed, she rocked it. She just sat there and stared at Alvin real hard for a long time, letting him know with that look in her eyes that she would never call him "father," or in any way was he going to replace her real daddyJabo.

To add insult to injury, she mucked her lips and asked him, "Where is your other family?"

The poor man didn't stand a chance, and could hardly keep his composure until Carrie said, "Neeyla, I done told you you're grown and need to mind your own business."

On that note, Neeyla rattled spoons, knives, and forks, and angrily absented herself from the table.

Alvin maintained his sense of humor and stated, "That's a tough one there."

We all just laughed, knowing it was truth. Then he confided in us that his family had been killed tragically, and then we felt sorry for him, for sure. Alvin indulged and lavished his supper as if it were a meal fit for a king. He talked a mile a minute over his rice and gravy, greens, and cornbread, the whole time telling us about his many expeditions. He had this peculiar way of saying "been knowin'," as if he were the only person to truly know about a thing or a situation. He was possibly the wisest man in the world with "been knowin'."

After Carrie started to cut up the deep, rich green watermelons he'd bought for us to enjoy later that night, he said, "Carrie, y'all know that these are the sweetest watermelons that you can eat. I raised and picked these myself in a big ole ditch. Carrie, when I was a young boy growing up on a farm in Carroll County, my paps showed me how to grow sweet watermelons. Hmm, hmm, been knowin'," he kept saying as he downed large pieces of fleshy watermelon.

His favorite pastime was watching *Soul Train* on Saturday nights. He would just sit there in a trance as the young girls twirled their booties across the stage, while putting his hands on his forbidden places.

This incensed Neelya even more, and she would roll her eyes and quietly say, "It ought to be a law against these old men and their wandering eyes." Carrie didn't mind, though. For once in her life, she had someone that she could at least talk to without going to all-out war, and sometimes we would still catch them hugging and kissing just like they used to when we would peep through the door window. Although he wasn't our real daddy Jabo, he was just fine, and often brought cheer to our evenings with his many and varied fabricated tales of which Carrie would often tell him to quit lying. To this day, I can still see his sincere smile reveal an armful of love for his beloved, and that first time he came home to dinner with us. By the time I entered high school, they had become husband and wife.

CHAPTER 6

# WC WILLIAMS SCHOOL

WC Williams was no longer a building that we passed on the way to school; it became an essential part of my daily experience.

Neeyla kissed me on the forehead and told me that she loved me. Suddenly, I was thrust into the halls of education, whereby which I would learn to stand and function as an independent and capable being. That day she dressed me in a lovely little orange shirt and matching brown pants with bright orange yarn ribbons in the same autumnal tones. We were all ushered into the auditorium, where we would be introduced to our home room teachers.As the presenter welcomed each of us to the new school year, I felt a flutter of butterflies erupt and explode in my stomach as my named was called to stand with Mrs. Crow, who would be my first grade teacher. I quietly eased from my seat and joined the ranks of what would be my future graduating class.

After all of my classmates were called to Mrs. Crow's homeroom class, we quietly strolled through the grass and across the narrow walk to her classroom. The room was tidy, scholarly, and oozing with chalkboard dust as she assigned our seats. I was fortunate enough to have a seat across the second row, close to the teacher's desk.

She then showed us her daily rules, which were plastered across the top of the chalk board. We would have to say them every time someone violated one of them.

"Good morning, students. I am Mrs. Crow, your first grade teacher," she stated in a husky, aging voice. Each day we would begin with a morning prayer and the pledge of allegiance to the flag. "Let's practice it now. Stand and place your left hand over your chest, raise your right hand, and repeat after me: 'I pledge allegiance to the flag of the United States of America, and to the republic for which it stands, one nation under God, indivisible, with liberty and justice for all.'"

Mrs. Crow's face foretold that see had seen better years, and was far past her prime. She was a mean faced cross-eyed looking woman who looked like hell frozen over. Her very name called attention to her long, beaked nose and deep set eyes which became the essence of recess taunts. Afterwards we were issued a basal reader we would read from each day. However, I thought the basal readers lacked luster, since Neeyla had already introduced me to *Gulliver's Travels* though the Golden Classics she would buy me at the Five and Ten Cent store when she had extra money. Each day we started and ended in the same routine as the day before, until some of my classmates decided that they would spit spitballs across the room to relieve the boredom.

"Well!" Mrs. Crow shouted. "When the bell rings, do not dare move!"

She kept us until Neeyla accosted the classroom door, saying, "I came to pick up my baby, Tracy Sandifer."

One look at Neeyla made Mrs. Crow know that she meant business. Now, since Neeyla was growing into her early twenties, she carried with her expression a look of sincere solemnity and a don't-mess-with-me attitude. Besides that, Neeyla's hair was sitting high upon her head in a big ole fro, and after one look at her, Mrs. Crow said, "Tracy, you may be dismissed."

Neeyla used to walk Davis and me to school since a neighborhood outcast, who we called D-man, resided on the far end of the street, cornedbetween WC Williams and Sunlight groceries. Neeyla called him this outlandish name because he often stood in his doorway stark buck naked, with a long ponytail. The very presence of him was enough to send a child into a reverie of nightmares. He was a very menacing figure who looked to be about fifty years old, and usually did not wear either a shirt or pants or underwear, for that matter. We often ran past his house at top speed in sheer terror for fear of being dragged into his house. We would often hear loud machinery coming out of the back of his house, and was certain that a poor girl's body was probably being cut in a million pieces. Some days when Neeyla had to work, and could not meet us at the cross walk, I would thus prepare my heart to make a mad dash across the crosswalk.

Suddenly, on one such occasion, a quick glance at the open screened porch brought me face to face with a buck naked shadowy figure, who motioned me with his winking eye. That moment, my heartbeat faded, and an inaudible cry found its way to my lips as I gathered my senses and ran the short distance home, crying and screaming, full speed down the sidewalk. I somehow ran directly through the front door crying. "Ahh! Ahh! Momma!"

"What's wrong, Flippadiddy?" questioned Grandma.

Neeyla immediately grabbed me and asked if someone had been fighting on me. Between sobs and tears, I said, "That white man was naked and winking his eyes at me."Before Carrie could grab Neeyla, Neeyla grabbed her purse and Jabo's hammer. "I'll teach that damn pervert to mess with my child, a funky bastard!"

Carrie shouted, "Neeyla, do not go down there! You don't know what that bastard has."

"Move, Momma. This is my child, and if he wants to show his thang, he gon' show it to me today."

Before Carrie could get another word out, Neeyla was charging down the street, running full speed. "Bring your nasty ass out, pervert! I'll show you to fuck with my child! I know you're in there. Come out, pervert!"

The door slowly opened as others from the neighborhood gathered in the front yard. By this time, Neeyla was railing at top of her breath. "She's all I got!"

The police officers, in a flurry of blue lights, quarried around the front door in a bustle of questions. "Is there a problem here?" asked the tall officer.

"It sure is!" yelled Neeyla. "This ass was showing my daughter his thang, and winking his eye at her."

"Sir, she is overreacting. I had my shirt off after making it in from work."

"You are a lying bastard," said Neeyla as she brandished the hammer at him. "I'll hit your ass right between the eyes."

"Ma'am, put that hammer down before you end up in jail with him. Sir, I need you to come down to the station with me," said the officer. "Ma'am, do me a favor, calm down, and take yourself and that hammer back home. Trust me. You won't have this problem again."

That night, visions of sheer nightmares flooded my thoughts, as I was thinking that if he went to jail and got out, he was sure to kidnap me or Neeyla while either of us was going to the store. I was sure that we would end up being cut up and lost forever in his backyard cemetery. After that incident, I was never allowed to walk home anymore, and had to wait on my uncle and aunt. Sometimes Senator Justice would stand right there at the crosswalk, dutifully watching generations of children turn away at the sound of the school bell back into their own neighborhoods.

Spring time finally came, and the children romped against the backdrop of densely woven clover grass and blossoms as they played dogged games of momma, teacher, and doctor.

Moray, my best friend and classmate,spoke in the muted quiet tones of a six year old who was ready to embrace the adventures of the blazing sun. “When I count to ten, all children must line up and not say another word.”

The children laughed derisively until they heard the bell, which was accompanied by Mrs. Montgomery’s plastic-sounding voice and the all-too-familiar, “Recess is over. Line up, children, and do not say another word.”

Of course, we would quietly stump the grass as we laughed on the inside at Mrs. Montgomery’s monotone voice like an eager army of fourth grade ants marching back to the dismal barracks of education.

Mrs. Montgomery, our reading teacher, had a face like a storehouse mannequin, fine, well-placed features, too, with dark-brown eyes. She even dressed in nice woolen sweaters with real pretty flowing skirts. That woman had to have been handmade by God Himself, with no parents in the process.

Each day we would go through the same routine for the entire nine months of school, just as we always did. Only in Mrs. Montgomery’s class, one felt welcomed and not like a hostage tied up against a wall. She was gentle in her dealing with the students, not harsh and demanding. Learning was not routine, but lively and engaging. In her quiet teacher’s voice, she would start the day with a writing warm up. We had to copy five cursive sentences from the handwriting model book into our primers daily. This was where I learned the handwriting that I have to this day. The reading lesson would always follow behind writing.

"Students, our reading lesson for this week is 'Country Mouse, City Mouse.'"

Morayyelled out, "What is it about?"

"Raise your hand, and I will tell you what it is about. All listen quietly. Long ago, there were two cousin mice. One lived in the city, and one lived in the country. The city mouse decided to pay his country cousin a visit in which he was indulged in all of his favorite cuisines."

"Mrs. Montgomery, what are cuisines?" asked the eager-eyed children. "We will learn them in the context of the story," she replied.

A unison of hands reached high as the ceiling. "Can I read? May I read? Me, Me, Me!" called my peers from their desk. With a calm purveyance of her class, Mrs. Montgomery called on Jeffery Wimbley to read. Jeff was usually not paying any attention in class, and would be the last one to raise his hand to read anything, so that made him chief target to be called on. With a shrug of his shoulders, Jeff slowly read by forcing the words to come out of his somewhat shamefaced cheeks and lips. Mrs. Montgomery told him to sit up straight and pronounce his words clearly, and then volunteered me to continue reading the next two pages of the text.I began, "Now you must know that a town mouse, once upon a time, went on a visit to his cousin in the country. He was rough and ready, this cousin, but he loved his town friend, and made him heartily welcome. Beans and bacon, cheese and bread, were all he had to offer, but he offered them freely. The town mouse rather turned up his long nose at this country fare, and said, 'I cannot understand, cousin, how you can put up with such poor food as this, but of course, you cannot expect anything better in the country. Come you with me, and I will show you how to live. When you have been in town a week, you will wonder how you could ever have stood a country life.' No sooner said than done, the two mice set off for the town and arrived at the town mouse's residence late at night. 'You will want some refreshment after our long journey,' said the polite town mouse, and took his friend into the grand dining-room."

CHAPTER 7

# SATURDAY WASH DAY IN GANGSTER'S PARADISE

Saturday wash day came, and we, along with Grandma Carrie, packed and pulled soiled laundry from forgotten and forbidden places, and packed them into waiting laundry baskets sprawled across the hallway.

Saturday wash day was a typical day to be both abhorred and detested by the adults, but for us children, it was a day riddled with both adventure and the merriment of putting new silver coins in the washer and dryer chute, and waiting for the sudsy release of the intricate battle of both suds and grim as the wash cycle gave up its final conquest. While Saturday wash day bought its own wonder and adventure, the trip to Gangster's Paradise held wonders that eyes could not phantom. Henry Street laundromat was in the heart of GP. GP, a community of shanty homes, was once considered to be the most impoverished part of the city of Greenwood.

As we rode through this forbidden section of town, Carrie would often scold Oscar for his meanderings in GP, of which he would often resolutely deny. "I ain't been in no GP. They telling lies on me."

Henry Street itself embodied the dissension of poor suffering souls who had succumbed to the backlash of urban unemployment. As we drove, slowly making our way to the laundromat, I witnessed teens in huddled masses who were affirming their stance through corruption, crimes, and gang violence, standing in a huddle under an old tree directly across the laundromat. This sad spectacle paid homage to not only poverty, but to plain old despair and ugliness. The ground itself was barren, void of dreams, hopes, and aspirations, and spoke multisyllabic expressions of the plight of the aged, oppressed, and intolerant. The stigma associated with the name Gangster's Paradise cried from beneath blind bullets, cries in the night, drunken stupors, girls having unprotected sex, and night profanities. Gangster's Paradise mocked back at poverty by regrouping and reassembling itself in an all-out war. Only this time, it was not against a society that had encapsulated and spellbound them.

Only this time, it was not against Jim Crow or the residue of slavery. Only this time, it was gang violence that pierced through the community with self-sabotage and degradation. The teens had traded the massa's whip for a game of broken dice, deuces wild, and Russian roulette while flanked across the backside of forsaken and decrepit places in their community. For a rhythmic dance of belonging, they had traded the March to Freedom, the journey across the Atlantic in cramped quarters, the lament and wails of the Negro slave spirituals, and the whiplash of oppression. They had traded all of these things given to them by their ancestors, and at a 360-degree angle, fired a single bullet into their brother's brain. Even as a child, I intrusively knew that the teens had become their own worst enemies trying to mask their fears against their failures.

As I stood there peering out the window, Carrie's voice gripped me with its sternness back into reality. "Flipadidy, come away from that window and help Eloise fold these towels. Flipadiddy, get over here and stop that daydreaming."

Only I wasn't daydreaming at all, I was questioning a broken reality. Sure enough, I hopped to it, for folding the towels on Saturday wash day was the best part. Eloise would dole out the little wash towels and hand towels to me while she folded the big towels into high, neat stacks of multicolored mounds.

"Flipadiddy, what were you over there thinking about?" she questioned me.

"I was just thinking about all those boys that be under that big tree, and how Oscar might be running with them," I explained.

"Thinking about them for what?" she questioned.

"I was just thinking about how they be out there all the time, every time we come here."

Eloise sharply stated, "Keep your butt away from there, staring at those GP boys, before you get your little ass shot in the face. Those are gangs, and this is GP, and that's enough for you. I damn meant it."

For a long time, I just stared my aunt dead in the face until she tightly gritted her teeth, letting me know not to say anything else.

Of course, the best part of Saturday morning wash day before heading back home was Sammy Waterly's Grocery store. After Carrie and Jabo separated, Carrie continued to work as a domestic for Mrs. Baker's friend in North Greenwood. She had become acquainted with Sammy while working for the Buergermots. Sammy, a relative of the Buergermots, was a pot-bellied man in his early sixties. Sammy was a World War II veteran who had certainly seen his share of tragedy. He had remarried Miss Ellie, a fair-faced blond twenty years his junior.

Miss Ellie always marked her day with smiles, and had a natural disposition toward friendliness and patience, whether clearing out the grocery tab, or keeping the store tidy, or just supporting Sammy in his many wiles. She did it with all smiles. Sammy's children from his first marriage and his wife were all around the same age.

Some weekends when we went to the store, we would see Henry Baker sitting at the back of the store with his cousins. He just peeked out at Neeyla and pretended he didn't see her. To their union, Sammie and Miss Ellie had three small children, with the youngest being around five years old. It had gotten around the town, and was rumored that Ellie's last child looked a great deal like Sammy's son by his first wife. Well, I'm not saying this was rumored right, but I'm not saying it was rumored wrong either. Well, let the cookies fall where they may, because that was between Sammy and Miss Ellie. Hell, if they wanted to keep it all in the family, then just let them. Miss Ellie always treated us nice, so I ain't mad at her.

In his post retirement years from the military, Sammy had taken up selling and crediting grocery to those who were trying to make their ends meet and feed their families. I can still remember our first trip to Sammy Waterly's Groceries with such poignant memories. Brown burlap sacks of flour and meal sat strategically throughout the aisles, with some in tall metal cans that looked like trash cans. Multitudes of sorghum molasses and Blackburn's syrup sat on the handmade shelves, suggesting the quiet aroma of Saturday morning breakfast with smokey sausages and scrambled eggs. Open freezers of home-cured country ham, neck bones, hog jowls, and bacon engulfed the atmosphere, sending hungry souls on an imaginary feast. Red Magnolia sausages poked out in massive links and recurled themselves against the white encrusted freezer. There were stacks of lunch meat loaves, fresh salami, bologna, hog head sauce, and sharp cheddar cheeses with bright orange casings.

When Carrie's basket was deemed overflowing with meat and grocery sufficient to feed her family for the duration of the month, we accosted both Sammy and Miss Ellie's smiling countenances, and they were always glad we'd come. The delicious Smiling Jack's cookies adjacent to the counter filled our childhood fantasies with sugar plum fairies dancing in our heads. Fat peppermint sticks, Chick-O-Sticks, Mr. Goodbars, PayDays, orange slices, and gum drops sat there for the taking, of which Carrie grabbed a couple sacksful, which would be rationed out to us to both indulge and appease our sweet tooths if we had eaten all of our vegetables.

That night, after a long day at the laundromat and grocery store, Carrie made homemade burgers and fries. The house smelled like Lucy's Cafe, seething with fresh fried onions, pungent black pepper, and brown toasted buns placed generously over pleasingly plump hamburger patties. Only back in those days, Grandma had seven children to feed and a new grandbaby on the way since her daughter Luella had gotten pregnant in the eleventh grade, so she would add some white bread to her ground beef patties just to make it stretch. I just think that all that extra bread was making them fat as heck.

After supper, we all gathered in the front room, sharing and recollecting ghost tales, the Sandifers' favorite pastime. Of course, the Money Road would always take center stage in our many ghost tales.

Neeyla said, "Do y'all remember that black silhouette that appeared in the window when we were out there living by the broadcast station on the Money Road?

Funny thing, this full apparition didn't even bother to remove itself with cars passing by with bright lights. We were scared as heck, and Jabo, who had been drinking, turned over and went back to sleep, telling us that we hadn't seen anything. That same night, it was raining and lightning torrents when the dark-red spot in the floor suddenly seemed to illuminate itself to a brilliant bright red. Carrie had tried with all of her might to get that blood stain out of the floor. She had used bleach, lye, and ammonia—you name it—but to no avail. I guess that was just that poor man's blood crying from the ground, since the house had once been a juke joint where he was killed in the very room over a gambling debt.

Then Eloise, without announcement, said, "I am sho glad we got the hell away from there, with all them damn haints, and us scared to go to sleep at night."

Carrie gritted her teeth at her, saying, "Didn't I tell you to stop all of that damn cussing?"

Eloise glared back at her like she wanted to cuss again, but Carrie's stare, and the back of her hand, silenced all thoughts of foolishness.

CHAPTER 8

# OAK STREET: FOR BETTER

With Neeyla now working full time at Rocky Manufacturing, she could now afford a place of her own, and secured a one-and-a-half bedroom home in East Greenwood.

The little house sat on raised concrete pillars in a community of shotgun facsimiles identical to their counterparts yet different. After all, Neeyla had placed an air conditioner in the window, and, well, that just gave hers an air of defiance. On the outside, the house was covered with mint-green roofing singles, and had a concrete porch that was big enough for some of Neeyla's family to gather, that led straight inside the living room. The living room was painted a soft, muted shade of ivory, with the remainder of the three rooms being plain off-white and in need of a fresh coat of paint. However, Neeyla didn't mind that, since she could get Archibald's best friend Martin to paint it for her for a nominal fee.

Neeyla had been working for a while, and had saved enough money to purchase a burgundy leather living room suite and matching dark-brown end tables. Boy, we were high flaunting with all that leather furniture.

"Momma, I like it," I said, and inquired as to whether I could play in the grass and flowers once we completely moved in.

"As long as you don't venture out of the yard, or try to go across the street, you can play out there."

"Yes, ma'am," I returned in sheer delight since I had already spotted some buzzing honey bees and little lavender flowers growing between the folds of the grass. These, I imagined, would be a source of wonder and merriment for hours on end, since even back then, science and its wonders of nature held me in fascination of its countless mysteries.

It was during this time that I noticed my momma had a strange glow in her cheeks and a magic sparkle in her eyes. She had begun to play her favorite love song, "Hypnotized," over and over again as loud as she could play it, probably waking up the whole neighborhood, including the dead. I knew that she was thinking about a man, but which one? Neeyla had had three boyfriends at one time that I knew of. I'm sure she wouldn't mind me telling this, because she was not ashamed at all.

One time, when she thought that I was asleep, I really wasn't; I stayed up on purpose to see why Neeyla's bed was shaking like that at night.

I tiptoed out of my bed that night when it started just to see what was really going on, because I had seen some of Neeyla's nasty books. As I stood in the doorway, I heard them saying, "Ooh, baby, I love you so."

In a slightly audible child's voice, a small cry of "Ooooh!" emanated from my throat, and Neeyla became very quiet and sat straight up in the bed.

Upon close inspection of my shadow in the door, she shouted, "Get your little narrow behind back in that bed!"

I was caught empty handed, and ran quickly back to my bed, and put all the covers over my head, sticking and pouting my bottom lip out well into the next day. From that moment on, I decided that man Miquel was no friend of mine. She had quit her other two boyfriends for him, a tall, slender, playboy-looking teacher named Miquel Tolarrie. Grandma Carrie hated the looks of him, and called him "Possum Face," since his face was narrow at the bottom like a possum's. Of course, by then, Eloise, Oscar, and Luella were running with the nickname Possum Face, and laughed every time at the mention of it.

Grandma would often ask me after school if Miquel had been over the night before. I told Grandma everything, like, "They be saying, 'Oooh, baby, I love you' in the bed every night." Grandma's face turned purple and she said that she was going to tell Neeyla a thing a two. She said that Neeyla didn't need to be having no more babies by another man with no husband.

That night, I promptly told Momma what Grandma had said, and for the next few weeks I had to stay with an elderly neighbor after school, and would not be going to Grandma's house for a while. From that moment on, I learned to keep my big mouth shut. Mrs. Aggie was a sixty-seven-year-old widow, whose house looked fairly clean but smelled like rat piss. She had no children of her own, and cherished the company of a small child. Every day she would try to offer me soup and neck bones. As Neelya and I passed her house on the way from school each day, she would often tell Neeyla how much she had wanted to have children of her own, and that she would babysit me free of charge if Neeyla wanted to go to nursing school. Only thing was, Neeyla didn't have her mind on no books, the least bit. She was too busy running behind playboy Possum Face.

It looked to me like she was trying her best to make another baby, like Carrie had said. And I didn't want no little brother or sister, for that matter. I was the only child, and as far as I was concerned, that was the way it was going to be. Miquel would promptly show up at the same time most days when he left his job at Lexington State

University, where he worked as an associate professor of sociology. When he saw me, he would pick me up and give me a nasty wet smack dead on my face, to which I said, "Ugh!" and wiped it off as hard as I could. The truth was, I didn't like him. For one thing, he was always kissing Neeyla in her mouth, and squeezing on her. After all, Neeyla was my mother.

Late one Friday evening on Valentine's Day, he came carrying heart-shaped boxes of Russell Stover's candies and big bouquet of fragrant yellow roses surrounded with tiny white baby's breath. He winked his eye at me and motioned me to sit on his knee. Then he asked me, "Where is Neeyla?" I told him that she was in the kitchen cooking, and baking a red cake. He then handed me the smaller box of candies and said, "Happy Valentine's to you, little one."I then decided to give him one of my Valentine's cards from school. He smiled and told me that he and Neeyla were going to be married the following week at the court house, and that he was going to be my new father. I just sat there and stared at him for a long time, wondering why he was going to be my new father when I really didn't need a new one at all, since Neeyla and I were fine without one. I thought to myself that Grandma was sure to put an end to this when she found out, and I would just wait until after school to tell her. That night at the kitchen table we ate pepper steak, whole potatoes, and strawberry cake. I sat quietly in the corner, making imaginary trails in my plate. Neeyla gave me a firm look and told me to eat my food.

The following Saturday, Neeyla and Miquel were married at the courthouse before the justice of the peace. Aunt Reena and her boyfriend, Uncle Adebiyi, came home from Chicago that weekend to attend the ceremony. After we walked into the courthouse, we walked down a long corridor and were accosted by a tall, blue-eyed gentleman in a black Sunday suit. He did a double take, and then loudly stated, "Why, if it ain't Neeyla Jean!"

Neeyla turned with a look of startle and surprise on her face. "Henry Baker, is that you? You back here?"

"I sure am. Somebody's gotta run this town. Girl, I done had three babies, two sons, and a daughter since I graduated from law school. We moved back to Money and renovated Momma's old house a few years after the storm. That tornado destroyed everything and nearly leveled that place. I thought about y'all for the longest, and wondered where you'd moved to. Why, Neeyla Jean, I be damned, you still got it!"

Neeyla blushed and said, "Henry, this is my fiancé, Miquel, my cousin Reena, and Adebiyi, my sister Luella, and her baby,Dashani ."

"Nice meeting y'all. I'm Henry Baker."

"Hello, I remember you," said Reena, laughing loudly.

"And you know who that little one is," said Neeyla.

"How could I forget? You were mean as a rattlesnake and big as a house while you were carrying her, but you sure stole Momma's heart. You were all she talked about. Neeyla, that girl is the spitting image of you. Y'all look nice. Where you heading?"

"We looking for the justice of the peace. Miquel and I are getting married."

"Get out of here, Neeyla! You done snagged you one. Congratulations, man, and nice meeting y'all. Well, I'm headed to court. However, the justice of the peace is the second door on the right once you go through them double doors." He reached into his pocket and retrieved a business card, and gave it to Neeyla. "Neeyla, call me. It's about some things I found at Momma's that belong to you."

"I will, and good to see you again, Henry Baker."

We soon learned that Henry was a local attorney who was running for district judge. However, many years would pass before Neeyla would retrieve what was left to her by Mrs. Baker.

Soon we stood face to face with the justice of the peace. They repeated some words after him, and at the end, gave each other a long lustful kiss that I thought was just plain ole nasty at that time. Aunt Reena was right by her side, and I could tell that she was crying both tears of joy and sadness for Neeyla. Somehow Reena had always felt responsible for Neelya getting pregnant, since she had led her to that juke joint where Roscoe was playing in the first place. Reena gave Neeyla a crystal punchbowl and some monogrammed towels with her new name, Tolarrie, on them, along with some new dresses and ponytail holders for me. She and I spent most of Saturday afternoon reading together and braiding my hair. Later that evening, they played cards in the backyard and listened to music while Reena, Luella, and Adebiyi danced to the beat of the music. She was the color of warm coffee, and wore her hair piled high up in a love knot.

Not long after their marriage, we moved out of town. The beginning of summer found us living on Union Street in Nettleton, Mississippi. Miquel, Neeyla, and I had moved over two hundred miles away from home. Neeyla gave up her dreams, hopes, aspirations, and traded it all for a phony two-dollar bill. Carrie said that she went running to the end of the rainbow looking for a treasure she never found. The infidelity, of course, had started long before we made the long trip to north Mississippi in Miquel's Gran Torino. By then, Miquel's tongue had turned into a burning arsenal of insults toward Neeyla, who was gradually fading into a shadow of herself. She had long stopped caring about her personal appearance, and her once well-groomed bushy mane would stand on ends uncombed for days.

A heated argument ensued one evening after Neeyla questioned his whereabouts. "Miquel, where are you going this time of night?" she questioned.

"Don't question my whereabouts, because where I'm going, you can't go. Now is that enough answer for you?"

"Never mind, since I know you gon' be with yo hoes tonight, you lying bastard. I found all them pictures of your sluts you sleeping with under my bed. How could you?""Why your fat ass snooping through my personal belongings? I done told you to keep your nose out of my personal business."

"You don't have any business, funky whore!" Neeyla screamed loudly at him.

This last insult resulted in a hurl of licks being passed back and forth. Neeyla had discovered that Miquel had recently been dismissed from his job at the university for having sexual relations with his students, which had ended in a trail of venereal disease. Of course, she found out that he was the carrier, in addition to the fact he had recently been stripped of his teaching license for his misconduct. The handsome, beautiful man who she loved more than life itself had hurdled her dreams into the deep abyss of disillusionment. Neeyla cried herself to sleep that night, and I hugged her close to console her.

During our visit to Grandma's, Grandma asked, "Neeyla, why you walking around here looking slouchy like that?"

Neeyla smarted, "Get you some business."

"You are gaining weight and not taking care of yourself. I told you not to marry that possum-faced, dope-smoking bum."

Neeyla managed to say between sobs, "Well, that's just too bad, but it's already done now. Besides, I quit my job today, and Miquel and I are moving to Nelleton, Mississippi, Saturday."

A wall of tears swelled up in Carrie's eyes. She tried her best to hold back the inevitable and the fear that Neeyla and I would never return. "Why you taking my grandbaby out there with that man? Because, if you ask me, I don't think that he cares anything about you."Neeyla raised her brows and said, "How you gon' tell me who to be with, when you stayed right there with my daddy Jabo for over twenty years, and all he did was beat you black and blue?"Grandma didn't say another word. She just stared away in silence for a long time. hoping that the silence would eat up the pain.

CHAPTER 9

# NETTLETON: FOR WORSE

When we arrived in Nettleton, my first singular impression of it made me think about the fishing lakes that Neeyla and Miquel had so frequently visited, which I hated with a burning passion. They would go fishing so much that after a while I just stopped getting out of the car, and would crouch down in the backseat whenever a cow or a goat happened to pass by. Our house, which was a little more than a shotgun, was across from the main highway. At night, the cars would fly by in the dark, and Neeyla told me that it reminded her of the Money Road that we had lived on so long ago in Money, Mississippi. Since I had been too young to remember it, she would often tell me that Mrs. Baker's spirit was always watching over us whenever she became nostalgic and lonely.

Union Street our new home, which looked to me like the middle of nowhere, but soon caught my fancy, since there were lively patches of raspberries and blackberries growing in deep mounds on the far edge of our backyard. However, Neeyla told me that I couldn't eat them because she couldn't tell what they actually were. I found sheer delight in just plucking the ripe fruit and just imagining if they tasted like the ones that Eloise, Oscar, and I enjoyed when we lived on East McLaurin, our first house in Greenwood. My real pleasure was making the tadpoles squirm that I had discovered in an old abandoned washing machine in the backyard. As the weeks rolled by, I slowly watched them grow into tiny, green slimy frogs that would jump in and out of the washing machine at their leisure, until one day they were all mostly gone.

When Neeyla and Miquel went to work, I often stayed at the home of Mrs. Jena Springer. Mrs. Springer looked like she was at least one hundred years old, a slender, erect, pretty-faced woman with long and mostly graying salt and pepper hair. Her house boasted an acidic vinegary smell since she always washed her hair in apple cider vinegar, saying it kept it long and healthy. I told Neeyla that I never wanted that stuff in my hair because it stank to high heaven. She smiled and told me not to worry. Mrs. Springer was Miquel's great aunt who had taught music at the elementary school many years ago. The first day I met her, she proceeded to show me her huge collection of hand-sewn stuffed cats that she'd created from pieces of multicolored fabric that she and squat niece would sew for hours on end. It appeared to me that there were countless hordes of them in almost every room of the house, boasting their smiling Cheshire cat faces in a homemade mausoleum. The larger cats were overstuffed with cotton and looked like a push pin would let the air out of them. When it was discovered that I could also sew by hand Mrs. Springer gave me a gray calico pattern of a large cat to follow. I then told her that my Grandma Carrie had taught me to sew by hand when I turned seven. She later informed me that I could sew on it each day if I promised to spend each afternoon with them, since I would often sneak back home across the yard to play with the tadpoles. Besides, they were both too old to even rationalize keeping up with my whereabouts, so I just randomly wandered back and forth between both houses just as I pleased.

Miquel and Neeyla were not arguing as much since Neeyla didn't bother to question his infidelity anymore, even when he started dallying with a young, thick-boned girl who was even younger than Neeyla, and lived right down the road from us. She was so brave that she actually had the audacity to send her daughter down the road to play with me. Of course, my friend one day told me that my stepdad was talking to her mother. I very casually announced, "So? Who cares," and we proceeded to play hopscotch, because deep down inside, Neeyla and I both treasured our time away when he was not there. We could at least have some peace.

One day Miquel came home and announced that since school would be starting in the fall, and his new job selling insurance was in Aberdeen, we would be moving the following week. I quickly gathered and transitioned my thoughts on what living in Aberdeen would be like, and whether Neeyla really wanted to move, because she had told me that Union Street reminded her so much of the Money Road. The following Sunday, after saying goodbye to Mrs. Springer and her niece, I said goodbye to my hidden patch of berries, green frogs, and handmade calico cats at the Springers. We traveled less than thirty minutes to Aberdeen, Mississippi, since the two towns essentially bordered each other.

Sunday evening found us neatly locked away in a long gray trailer that Miquel rented for thirty dollars a week. It was rather new, and had the appearance of a home away from home. I finally had my own bedroom, but was sorely afraid since my bedroom at our former home in Greenwood was on the near side of Neeyla's room. Neeyla told me that after she had been working a while that she would adorn it with Barbie doll pinks. However, this offered little consolation, because by this time, I was filled with phantasms and fear after a bad nightmare.

Well, I'm not one to air the family's dirty laundry, but Neeyla had gotten fed up with Miquel's running around, so she decided to rekindle her long time relationship with her former beau who was stationed in the military in Korea. He actually had proposed to her first, but one look at Miquel, and well, the rest was history. Anyway, Neeyla had written Lamuel and told him how unhappy she had become with Miquel, and about all his other women. He told Neeyla that he was scheduled to come home soon, and asked if he could see her again. Of course, Neeyla wholeheartedly agreed, and they agreed to a little rendezvous. Only Neeyla's little brother was always right behind her shirttail, and knew her every move. She had agreed to keep him for Grandma that day, who had been working a double shift at the Buergermots. He overheard her conversation, and later asked Neeyla if she could take him with her to see Lamuel because he always bought gifts home from Korea.

With an embarrassed look of startle on her face, Neeyla asked him, "Go where?"

He then replied, "With you and Lamuel."

She then told him, "You're not going anywhere, and I'm not neither."

He then said, "Hmm, hmm, I heard you."

After that, Neeyla told him to shut his face.

Later that evening, Miquel kept on questioning Davis about what Neeyla had been doing all day, since he was beginning to notice her changing attitude towards him. Of course, Davis, being a young child, told him everything. Miquel then made up his mind to watch Neeyla's every move. Sometimes after he went to work—well, he really didn't go to work. Oscar would spot him sitting in his car around the corner from the house just to watch Neeyla. Imagine that, with his ole possum-face self, and with all those women he had, and trying to watch somebody else. He tried his best to catch Neeyla, but for the record, Neeyla was way too smart to be outsmarted.

One Saturday when Miquel and Neeyla had gone fishing off of Blue Lake, he decided to confront her about her relationship with Lamuel. Of course, Neeyla, being Neeyla, decided to give him a taste of his own medicine.

"Neeyla, you been screwing around on me, giving my stuff to that other nigga, is you? You belong to me, and that's mine."

Neeyla looked at him and said, "The hell you preach. I don't see yo name on it, with your possum face."

Miquel screamed, "What did you say?!"

"You heard me. I don't see your damn name written on it."

Before she could scarcely get the words out of her mouth, Miquel slapped Neeyla down. After she got up and struck him back, he pushed her back down and proceeded to kick her violently in the face with his hard work shoes. The Lord works in mysterious ways, because while Miquel tried his best to end my mother's life on the Blue Lake that day, the Lord caused our cousin Hattie, who lived down the road, to pass by right in the midst of the violence. Hattie snatched Neeyla back from the death and destruction. She quickly parked her car on the side of the highway and ran to Neeyla, screaming, "Stop! Let her go before I shoot you down! Help her, Lord, help! Neeyla, are you all right? I got you, and bastard, if you lay another finger on her, I'll blow you to kingdom come."

By this time, he was scurrying away to his car, jumping in, digging up mud, and driving away because Hattie was known to carry a sawed-off shotgun in her truck, and wouldn't hesitate to use it. Neeyla had become almost incoherent, and Hattie grabbed her and dragged her to the car while blood poured from her face. It wasn't long before the entire family was in the emergency room wondering about Miquel's whereabouts. Hattie warned Neeyla that God had given her a way of escape, and that she best learn from her mistake. Both Carrie and Jabo called the law on Miquel, but Neeyla refused to press charges. We stayed at Grandma's for some weeks, and Grandma would not allow Miquel near Neeyla or her house, and had threatened to shoot him. Jabo said that if he caught Miquel walking anywhere, he was going to lay him low.

After the scars healed themselves and the pain went away, it was soon discovered that Neeyla had planned to agree to move out of town with Miquel, since she had said that after all, he was her legal husband. Grandma solemnly warned her, "Neeyla, don't be no fool." After hearing Neeyla and Miquel argue in the night about who knows what, I became afraid, reliving that awful beating that Neeyla suffered that day on the lake with Miquel. I imagined that he would take her away one day, and I would never see her again. Grandma begged Neeyla to come back home. So there we were, living in Nettleton, Mississippi, with **Neeyla burying her scars and covering them with a heavy woolen blanket into a deep nightmare of despair.**

Later, Miquel quickly became friends with the local community, and taught Sunday school like he was the nicest man on the planet. Sometimes he would act so differently at church that I hardly recognized him. One time I wanted to ask him, "Really?" It's funny how some people can parade and put up public fronts when they know they are nowhere near that at home. Don't they know that God is still watching them wherever they go? Of course, Neeyla would always ask me how he behaved at church, as well as how many women were there. I told her that they were all old and out of shape just to make her feel better.

It was nearly August, and I would be starting third grade at Nettleton Elementary School in a few weeks. Third grade unraveled itself in muted shades of motley colors and a forlorn look of exasperation in Neeyla's eyes. The elementary wing of third grade lay in deep shadows against the lovely backdrop of the school, and I very readily found my place among a sea of strangers in my new third grade class. The school itself reminded me a great deal of my former WC Williams.

The teacher greeted the class with an air of friendliness and dutiful servitude. We were all placed in alphabetical order, and quickly issued both social studies and English textbooks as she stated, "All lost textbooks must be paid for in the front office prior to the close of the school year."

I found solace in reading Medieval and enchanting tales of the new world with Christopher Columbus, the American Indians, the early American pioneers, and their first Thanksgiving in the new-found land. Homework consisted of recreating colorful pencil color drawings of the Niña, Pinta, and the Santa Maria, and various intricate world maps I would intricately labor over for hours. During recess we were also allowed to gather pine cones for our class turkey project, which would be completed before Thanksgiving. However, as things would have it, our Thanksgiving would be spent back in Greenwood.

Neeyla had not found employment in Aberdeen, so she had made the acquaintance of another of Miquel's great nieces, Shirley, who lived directly across the street from our trailer. I would often accompany her to Shirley's house after getting off the bus. Shirley's house reminded me of Mr. Melton's funeral home parlor in Greenwood, with its neatly lined mantles bearing numerous photos on the left side of the room, and a magic curtain that separated the front of the house from the living quarters. Shirley was a pie-faced woman with a small-framed adult daughter who looked like her identical twin sister. Only the girl never left the house, and would always run to the back when she discovered that we were there.

One day, Shirley told Neeyla that her daughter had gone off to college in Florida and become very ill in the middle of her sophomore year. She had boarded a train and cried all the way to Florida to be near her hospitalized daughter. She had forewarned Tillie, her daughter, who was on scholarship, about going to parties since she needed to use that time studying to keep up her grades for medical school. However, Tillie was not thinking about that, and was subsequently drugged by one of her so-called friends. Tillie was now twenty-five, fair of face, but virtually mindless. The doctors told Shirley that if Tillie lived, she would never be able to take care of herself. She simply sat straight up in her bed and stared into space all day when she wasn't completing crossword puzzles, knitting, or staring blankly at television reruns. I often tried to carry on conversations with her by asking her how her day had been. However, she simply stared straight through me, never saying a word. I asked Neeyla if she would be okay one day, and Neeyla said that God would heal her.

The days recolored and shaded themselves into the darker shades of fall, and Thanksgiving was poking its head around the corner. Neeyla had become accustomed to seeing me off to school, and in the afternoon, carrying on lively conversations with her new friend Shirley.

"Hey, Shirley, what you got going on?"

"Neeyla Jean, just tryna keep my head above water. Neeyla Jean, gul, why these men folk act the way they do? Ole dude said he was going call me last week, and I ain't heard nothing from him."

"Shirley, you know that man got a wife."

"Neeyla, he said they was separated."

"And you believed him?"

"Gul, I aint foolin' with you and these crazy men you messin' with."

"I know that's right." Shirley laughed. "Neeyla, you know that sour cream cake you been asking me about? Well, looka here. I found the recipe."

"Ah, shucks, looka here." Neeyla giggled.

It was closer to the holidays, so she and Shirley had started planning Thanksgiving meals. Neelya decided to begin experimenting with her new sour-cream pound cake recipe that she'd gotten from Shirley. It was Friday night, and I could stay up as late as I wanted to. That afternoon after school, Neeyla, Miquel, and I had gone grocery shopping, and Miquel had given me ten packs of king-sized Now and Laters in assorted flavors.

"Miquel, why you buy all of that damn candy? And why are you giving it to her? It ain't like you gon' take her to the dentist, because you can't even take your own self."

Neeyla must have been talking to herself because Miquel had already gotten his tweed jacket and slipped out the side door by the time she realized it. She instructed me to put some of it up, and not to eat too much of it. Afterwards, I assisted Neeyla with small tasks around the house while she prepared cake and meatloaf. My eyes darted back and forth as I watched Neeyla mix equal parts of cake flour, sugar, sour cream, 7UP soda, vanilla extract, real butter, baking soda, and milk, and blend it into a thick, creamy batter.

"Tracy, this is how you mix your batter," she explained, as she strategically placed the handheld mixers in my hand.

I watched in sheer delight as the frothy vanilla folds of cake batter refolded and redoubled on themselves.

"Ma, can I have the bowl?" I asked. This all too familiar phrase had echoed so often throughout Grandma Carrie's house in Greenwood as Davis and I had often debated who would get to lick the bowl or the mixing spoons while she prepared her delicious cakes from scratch.

The night progressed without event until Miquel's affectionate but arrogant poodle Pierre decided that he was not getting the attention that he deserved. Miquel was nowhere to be found, and Neeyla was teaching me how to bake a cake. He had been whining all that evening for Miquel, and Neeyla had scolded him to sit down and shut up. Pierre apparently had his own agenda. After the cakes had baked to desired consistency, Neeyla took them out of the oven and placed them on cake racks on the countertop to cool. Neeyla was sitting down to rest, engaged in *Sanford and Son*, and I had momentarily left the kitchen. Before I scarcely made it back, I spotted Pierre hunching over the counter, peeing on Neeyla's freshly baked cakes.

I screamed, "Ma! Pierre is peeing on your cakes!"

Neeyla hopped up from her seat, and running full speed to the kitchen, railed at the top of her voice, "What a filthy, evil-hearted little bastard, pissing on my cake!"Pierre charged full speed toward their bed, but Neeyla caught him in mid-air. The entire scene replays in my mind like the mighty feats of the circus acrobats. I was sure that Neelya was going to literally tear him to pieces, when suddenly Neeyla made a sharp turn to the bathroom, with him in full tow. She held his butt down in the toilet and literally flushed until I begged her to stop. My worst fear was that he would go down the toilet and drown, although this really was impossible. Neeyla wanted to train him that his behind was not meant for peeing on her cake.

This event brought our time in Nettleton to a short end, because Neelya told Miquel later that night that Pierre had done the unimaginable to her cake. Of course, Miquel had accused Neeyla of abusing his dog, and a huge fight ensued. Neeyla slept in my room that night and told me that Grandma Carrie and Alvin were coming, and we were returning to Greenwood.

The next day, her eyes were bloodshot during the long two-hundred-mile ride back to Greenwood. **She repressed the anger and resentment that the years had miscounted and miscalculated, and sent them on a journey of silence.** We moved back into Carrie's house, with Neeyla abiding by her rules. By the end of my fourth grade year, Carrie moved her family across town to Montjoy Street in the white folks' neighborhood, and Neeyla and I moved to GP (Gangster's Paradise.) **Carrie cringed, but Neeyla was on the road to self-discovery.**

CHAPTER 10

# LIVING IN GANGSTER'S PARADISE

Saturday Nights in Gangster's Paradise boasted a parade of drunken lovers reeking with musky Crown Royal and making mad drunken dashes in and out of the Fork Lounge.

The Fork Lounge was a mean and bawdy juke joint directly across the street from where we lived. Profuse profanities and flying beer bottles lay in scattered seas of refuse behind the club, glistening in the wee hours of the night. During the daylight hours, these images only magnified the dilapidated and downtrodden homes that resembled hulled-out shells burnt bare with decay. Most of the houses on our street had the same look of so many of the homes in the poorer sections of town. They, too, looked like tiny matchboxes stuck together with the windows cut out. I figured Neeyla had to be out of her mind for moving us into such a bad-looking neighborhood, but then again, she had given birth to me before her seventeenth birthday, so that was the best that she could do.

One night after Neeyla had gotten off from the late shift at the hospital, she spotted Lenny Summock, her new boyfriend, down on his knees trying to look up at a woman's privates who was squatting down in our front yard taking a leak. Of course, Neeyla promptly asked what the hell he was doing. However, we all knew that this sort of occurrence was no strange thing in our hood, and Lennie Summock was taking full advantage of it. When Neeyla walked in the house, she asked me what I was waiting on to go to bed. I told her that since I couldn't sleep, I was working on my papier-mâché sculptures for the art contest at school. She then told me to put it all away and get to bed for school the next day.

Our home was on the grounds of Wesley United Methodist Church, which was organized by the Freedman's Bureau in 1870. The church was originally built in 1921. It would ultimately be the church where I would become baptized. However, on the opposite end, across the street, was a spooky wall mural bearing a demonic image with a pitchfork in tow. It seemed to glare loudly as the music penetrated the walls of the neighborhood. The more the music jumped, the more it seemed to dance right on with. The thing scared me so bad that I didn't even like to walk on that side of the street in the daytime.

Late Friday nights, an iconic heroine of the night, Gustave Hewitt, the drunkest person you could ever meet, would stand at the corner of Gibb and Howard making vulgar and uncensored remarks as women with high heels and high behinds went in and out of the club. "Hey, pretty momma," he would slur between drunken lips.

"Get your ole ugly stankin' breath self out of my face, you drunk skunk."

"You ole bad body freak. I don't want none of that no way."

"Don't worry, drunk bum. I wouldn't touch you with a ten-foot pole, and I put that on my grandmamma."

He would make a face and suddenly turn and stagger aimlessly out of the club in search of any happenings that might venture his way. His first encounter with Neeyla made him learn to respect the power of a woman, and a cursing one at that. Neeyla must have been in her early thirties, but still had the youthful luster and appearance of a twenty year old, with high cheekbones and taut lips. She had once again become carefree, and it showed through and through. She had just arrived home from work late one night when Gustave accosted her.

"Mmm, hmm, look what I done found over here. Baby, where you been at all my life?"Neeyla gave him a piecing glare and stated, "I beg your pardon?"

He repeated, "Baby, where you been all my life?"

At the second mention of it, Neeyla reared way back in her hip and softly stated, "You got ten seconds to get your drunk, funky, dusty self out of my face, because if you don't, they gon' pick you up off this sidewalk in a million pieces. Now get the hell out of my face."Neeyla proceeded to reach into her large bag to retrieve what Gustave knew it to be."Ah, Ms. Neeyla, I didn't mean no harm," he said, as he glided quickly on down the sidewalk. When he was in what he thought to be a safe range, he yelled back down the sidewalk, "Baby, you still sho nuff look good to me, with your fine self. Ooooh wee!"

Neeyla just shook her head at him and laughed out loud to herself. From that moment on, they had an amiable level of mutual respect. Gustave never stopped making his vulgar advances at Neeyla, or any other woman, as far as that mattered. That was his way, and nothing was going to change that. However, we both discovered in time that hidden behind Gustave's drunken and vulgar tongue was a truly compassionate being who would actually stand up for any woman he felt was being mistreated. In fact, later in his old age, he actually preached on the same streets that he had wandered on, intoxicated, for so many years.

CHAPTER 11

# SANCTUARY: WESLEY UNITED METHODIST CHURCH

An air of nostalgia permeated the old church pews, the faithful alms of dutiful deacons and lovely women on the usher board who were the true pillars of the church.

The songs of Zion, fused with melodic voices, filled the sanctuary with a high-sounding soprano. Songs such as "Where You There?" and "Ezekiel Saw the Wheel" bounced back and forth in sharp echoes against the wall mural of the resurrected Savior and Mary Magdalene, and clashed sharply against the pitchfork-embossed neighboring café outside. The tune reveled in mockery against the forces without the walls of the church insinuating the final victory over sin and death, because God always has the final say, as I know and am told.

My godfather, Reverend Donald O'Jeffries' mighty arms would exalt the Heavens in a crescendo of adoration as he told us, "Hold to God's unchanging hand; build your hopes on things eternal." His well-adorned United Methodist clergical robe flowed mightily as he graced the pulpit. The O'Jeffries were the most dignified Blacks I knew in Greenwood, Mississippi. They had traveled from Columbus, Mississippi. Now Mrs. Connie O'Jeffries was just about the prettiest Black woman you would ever want to meet. She wore Jackie-O. empire dresses, just like Murtis, that flowed like satin drapes, and had doll feet beneath a well-built frame. Her cashew-colored skin glowed like a golden effervescent mist beneath the steady gait of her sincere smile. I took to her almost instantly because of her innate ability to connect with us children.

Although Connie O"Jeffries spoke softly, she carried a great big stick in her dealings with the children's ministry. She was sweet as pie, but we children knew not to play any games with her. As she moved about the sanctuary, her jaunty pin curls bounced in stride with the steps of a scholarly sophisticate. Once Connie married Reverend O'Jeffries, they lived for a while in Tupelo, Mississippi, before moving to the Delta, where they became pastor and first lady of Wesley United Methodist Church. Connie had taught home economics for many years, and was close to retirement. Reverend O'Jeffries had previously worked as a school principal, but was now a full-time pastor.

Sunday mornings at Wesley were infused with relics of the past that were resurrected each Sunday in sea of red hymnals and high octaves that burst and imploded the sanctuary, sending a mighty song of praise to the Heavens. These were the very songs that the slave ancestors had sang on their quest for freedom through uncharted territories that could kill the flesh but not the soul. Wesley United Methodist Church became a refuge that shielded me from the clutches and throws of the prevailing darkness and violence that surrounded my community. The church had been organized by the Freedman's Society shortly after the Civil War, with the building being erected about fifty years later. It had been a safe haven by which freed slaves could grow, build, and like Langston Hughes declared, "I, too, sing, America. I am the darker brother . . . " Indeed, the men and women of Wesley had not only learned to sing the songs of Zion, but had also created place in the very midst of barrenness and ugliness. Men and women who were solemn pillars of the community, a new breed of aristocrats, attorneys, physicians, professors, teachers, and social scientists who had made their own indelible mark on the face of history, were all gathered there in one accord. They were living witnesses who would not let nobody turn them around, and I, too, had become part of that reality.

At the age of fourteen, I came to know the Jesus of the Bible. For the first thirteen years of my life, I had not gone to church, with the exception of occasional visits with Neeyla, and Easter Sundays with Grandma Carrie. Nevertheless, I had always been taught to fear and revere God, since Grandma Carrie would not allow any sewing, washing, or major cleaning in her house on Sunday, for it was prayer that had saved my family from death as the violent tornado had ripped through Money, Mississippi, many years before.

CHAPTER 12

# HIGH SCHOOL

Fall came in fragmented shades of burnt umber and iridescent oranges.

The leaves were stuck to the trees like cockle burs to woolen sock, and school would let the children back in from a muggy and sweaty summer, slamming the outside doors with the full ringing of the morning tardy bell. It was the fall of 1983, and I would begin my high school career on the campus of Greenwood High School. Although I had caught an occasional glimpse of the high school each day during band practice, the first day of school would bring me face to face with classes, societies, and the full repertoire of the super sophisticates, the privileged higher-echelon girls and guys who wore dainty, stiffly starched shirts tucked into neat trousers and academy skirts. There was also the band squad; blue jean couture breezeway groupies; the for-crying-out-loud geek squad; the loud mouths and the tattle tails; and the crazy for no apparent reason. Today, as on other days, I held on firmly to the coattails of the band squad while they likewise marched to the beat of the super sophisticates who thought they were way more than what they were, when we all knew that they didn't have a pot to piss in. Thus unknowingly, we had formulated societies and tribe that somehow became intermingled and dispersed again during the course our daily routine.

The school itself sat squarely on its lone block of thirteenth-section land. Quick feet and the thud of determined gym shoes sailed down the hall in a feat of victory to conquer the tardy bell. Inside the classrooms were classes packed with summer-weary students held in restraint within the confines of long narrow corridors by fierce watchdog principals who stood towering at the ends of the halls. Wing A, or the main hall, boasted a wealth of teachers who had long borne the reputation of ripping the heart strings of the most intellectually astute. Mrs. Anne Coat's classroom on the far end of Wing A boasted a plethora of mid-century English literature, British authors of the twentieth century, red volumes of Merriam-Webster dictionaries, Charles Dicken's *Great Expectations*, and Shakespeare's *Macbeth*. The entire room was entwined in a deep reverie of enchanted tales stuffed in bareback books tucked away in tidy stacks on overcrowded bookshelves sagging in agony from overuse. Tidy quiet stacks of faraway tales from faraway places summoned and mocked the faint at heart. Neat teacher's scholarly posters sat squarely like pages in a well-groomed specialty shop. Each page in the teacher's roll book looked ironed out and flattened with use.

Mrs. Anne Coat had a reputation for making a believer out of the unrehearsed and undisciplined English learner. Mrs Anne Coat, a true icon of forgotten lore, glared solemnly from the behind the squared corners of her brown-colored bifocals. A neatly dressed demure woman in her early thirties, she smirked quietly as she passed out the English I syllabus to an awaiting army of wary pupils. After the last syllabus was given to the last student, she stated, "These must be returned signed by your parents before Wednesday of this week. Also, you will need a supply of typing paper, poster, ink pens, and college-ruled paper placed in a binder. No spirals, please. All notes are to be legibly written in ink, and kept in binders." Mrs Anne Coat herself looked like she had read over a million books in her life, and probably shouldn't be reading anymore.

After the first month of school, we had become accustomed to her daily dose of mental torment. For nine months, it loomed over us like creatures of the night in the form of a research paper that would stalk like the mighty cats of the jungle about to pounce on its prey. Anne Coat had earned her badge of honor long before any of us were born as the equalizer of any stubborn soul who refused to exercise his or her rights as an English learner. She was far all right. She just wanted to make sure her students got a free and appropriate education, whether they got it that year, or the next. They were bound to get it one way or the other.

One day,Anne Coat said, "Students, properly head your papers in accordance with the model on the chalkboard, and begin writing on the fifth line. In a few paragraphs, tell me some things about yourself and your summer vacation."

"Not again! And what do we need all this stuff for?" one student had the audacity to say, for this would be our third shot at retelling our summer vacation in first, second, and now third period class.

Suddenly, Mrs. Anne Coat peered at the student over the rim of her glasses for a while until he slipped down in his desk like a limp fish out of water. "Pardon me, is there a problem?" she spoke in well-articulated tones.

"Oh no, ma'am," was about all that he could muster up the nerve to say.

The entire class shook on the inside with laughter that they full well knew not to verbalize. The truth of the matter was that we were tired of hearing about our summer vacations ourselves, not to mention rewriting it for the third time. I even asked myself who in their right mind would want to read all of that stuff. The better half of it was probably made up, and if she followed them home, she would see an entirely different story. In fact, I wasn't trying to make up no fabricated lie about no summer vacation when the whole truth of the matter was that Neeyla couldn't afford to take us on no luxury summer vacations. Her job working as a certified nursing assistant was just enough to make ends meet. Yet somehow it was more than enough for us. Neeyla did her best to keep us from looking like we were byproducts of where we lived. Most of my friends were middle class, and lived in great big homes. Well, our apartment was small, but nicely furnished. Aside from that, Neelya made sure that my hair was always silk-pressed, and that I always had nice clothes to wear.

It was during this time that Neeyla had started dating Lennie Summock. Lennie, a burly man in his thirties, was a middle school math teacher who was a few years younger than Neeyla. Lennie loved telling jokes and recounting the adventures of his students during the course of the day. After they started dating, I was pretty sure that Neeyla had a thing for teachers. He and Neeyla would laugh out loud well into the wee hours of the night after watching hilarious episodes of Rudy Ray Moore's *Dolemite*. More than that, both Neeyla and Lennie like to indulge in exotic cuisine, and could turn even the most unsavory dish into a work of art.

On the weekends, we would ride up to Memphis, Tennessee, where our first stop would always be Piccadilly's. As soon as we entered Southland Mall, the aroma of Piccadilly's Cafeteria would hit us in the face. Neeyla and I would always have cod fish encrusted with almonds, crispy onion rings, and brussel sprouts dripping with cheese sauce, all of which we would wash down with syrupy sweet tea. After an indulgent meal, our first stop in the mall would be Gayfer's and McRae's makeup counter, where Neeyla would buy Estée Lauder Youth Dew and White

Linen for me. Neeyla said that Mrs. Baker would always give her Youth Dew during birthdays and Christmas. Mrs. Baker told Neelya that her husband Henry had adored the fragrance, and would always bring back gift sets of various Estée Lauder products. Neeyla had asked her why she was giving away her perfume. Mrs. Baker looked at her, smiled, and said, "Since he's always buying it, I'm always giving it away."

Out of all Neeyla's boyfirends, Lennie Summock was the only one that I even considered calling Daddy. He was full-bodied, like an athlete who had long dropped out of spring training. However, Lennie kept himself neat, and always wore white collared shirts, teacher's khakis, and happy neck ties. He and Neeyla had been friends for many years, since they were teenagers living on the Money Road. Way back then, Lennie was always giving her the eye and making motions with his tongue when she walked by. Of course, Neeyla was so busy courting Lamuel Lockran that she scarcely gave Lennie the time of the day. And now they were carrying on like they had been loving each other a lifetime. Imagine that!

Lennie's family was a member of the sanctified church on the far end of East McLaurin. Lennie had begged Neeyla to visit one Sunday so that she could attend his Sunday school class. She very curtly told him that she wasn't going to stop wearing no makeup, pants, or cussing. Though she had promised him that she would visit during a special program, we never did. On the other hand, I remained an active member of the United Methodist Church well into my twenties.

## CHAPTER 13

# PROM NIGHT

The sun waxed an alabaster glow in the sky; voices near and far yelled across the dimly lit gymnasium as they assembled the stage props for the prom. This year's theme was "An Enchanted Evening with the Stars," and Freddie Jackson's "Rock Me"" was playing in the background.

Silver foil stars were erected high and low on invisible pedestal stands against a midnight black sky. Aisles of clear black lights encased the entry way. The upperclassmen were in charge of set up, and the underclassmen were in charge of making it happen by ensuring that they had everything they needed. If you asked me, I would say that we were damn general flunkies. Run! Get this! Go get that! Who in the heck did they think they were? They were seniors, and we were right behind them. However, it was all in the name of love, because that night I would get to just stand there and gaze at my handsome honey, Weisman Richards.

Weisman would be attending the University of Mississippi in the fall to study engineering and psychology, so this would probably be the last time that we would see each other. The study of these two fields could be a great thing, since one could use this knowledge to study the study the assimilation of machinery, or how the parts were interrelated, but for him to go and study both engineering and psychology, now that was a whole different thing. Why would you need to study psychology to go and build things? Only thing I could figure was that one needed a sound mind to build a sound machine, is all I'm saying. Aside from that fact, his psychologist sibling wanted him to major in it.

All I know is that when I looked into them sexy eyes, my heart must have nose-dived twenty fathoms into the deep, only to revive itself and go back down there again. However, Neeyla had already told me that I was not courting, and if I got a baby, I would be the one who would rock it. In fact, this boy was like the moon, sun, and stars, all sitting in the sky at once, and to kiss his sweet honey-colored lips would be my fondest wish come true. But when Neeyla said that I couldn't have no boyfriend, she wasn't playing with me. Although she, . Of course at the time, I felt a little embarrassed but was quite accustomed to my Momma saying exactly what was on her mind.

Prom night came on April 20, 1986, and I stood at the door waiting for that sexy smile to pass my way. Almost instantaneously, he arrived at the table, waiting to be signed in with his date. Only she really didn't mean anything to him. Ole smear-face skank, standing there in all that pink, looking like a pint-sized bottle of Pepto-Bismol, and thinking she was God's gift to the world. I quickly signed them in and proceeded to say, "Next." She just stomped off, looking just plain old hand-me-down. They were just prom dates, and that was all. His eyes had already told me everything.

The students pranced from side to side. They danced to the beat of Prince's "Do Me, Baby," and shook their booties to Micheal Jackson's "Beat It." Against a tapestry of quick-silver stars, the upperclassmen came through flowing in a sea of silver and white gowns with pastels of translucents in between. The young men stole the show in matching white tuxedos, and my sweet thang danced round and round his pink bottle of Pepto. I just stood there and stared at them in disbelief, thinking to myself, *She dancing with my man.*

My classmates had often taunted me about being a virgin. "Girl, yo stuff so tight it's gon' kill you the first time," they mocked. Of course, I didn't have my butt on those dumb-sounding comments. I just smiled and said, "Oh well."

By this time, Weisman Stewart had gone off to Ole Miss to study engineering, and since we never even held hands, he was turning into a faint memory. On top of that, we had never even shared our first kiss, and besides, what did I know about love? Well, in truth, I was about to find out.

CHAPTER 14

# GRADUATION

Springtime revealed itself in a canopy of purple clover grass. The clear skies spoke solemn songs of aquamarine blues and sea greens while rolling back its lush canopy of purple clover grass, creating a song way deep down in my soul.

Wet dew tightly held the leaves of grass as I walked quietly across the civic center's walkway. My high school years were behind me, and I was fully arrayed in cap and gown, with matching honor cords. Graduation had granted me a full four-year scholarship to Rust College in Holly Springs, Mississippi, I had stared right in the face of obstacles, and overcome the common plight of my ancestors. The tiny baby who had been born to a teenage mother had dared to insult poverty and give it a swift backside kick into the abyss. My father would call sporadically, and childhood memories spent with him had faded into a distant blur. Neeyla told me he had married two more wives, and had two more sets of children after the first wife. I couldn't imagine anybody with that many women and children having time for anybody. Although I was Neeyla's only child, my siblings on my fathers's side and I would form inseparable and loving bonds in years to come.

Soon after graduation, I became acquainted with someone who would change the trajectory of my life forever. Well, he was certainly no sexy Stewart Wiesman; however, his expression foretold a look of innocence. Somehow we had connected. How? I do not fully understand. Raymir Gorman had recently graduated from college, and was now working as a journalist for a local newspaper. The first time that we'd met, he had asked me to go on a date with him. Of course, I flat out told him no the first time. A few weeks later, Neeyla told me to drop my scholarship announcement by the commonwealth office, and as fate would have it, that Raymir Gorman was sitting at the front desk.

"What you bringing yo ole self in here for? Won't give nobody no date," he said solemnly, then laughed. "What's that you got in your hand, girl?"

"It's my scholarship to Rust College, Raymir."

"You ain't won no scholarship. Besides, you look like you still in the tenth grade, and I ain't puttin' that bogus stuff in our newspaper. Well, only on one condition: If you promise to go out on a date with me, I'll put you on the front page."

I then asked him where he was planning on taking me on this date.

He laughed and said, "You look like a Burger King, have-it-your-way chick to me." Before I could call him a few four-letter words, Raymir then said, "Wherever your heart desires. Girl, I would take you to the moon and back if I could."

I casually announced that I would promise to go out on a date with him if he kept all of his hands to himself. He just looked at me and smiled that innocent smile. I must have been hooked from that moment on, for his eyes sparkled a magic sparkle of joy as they met mine.

Neeyla had worked the late shift that evening, so I decided to wait until the next day to tell her, since I had never been on a date. After school was out, I found Neeyla in the living room watching the *Days of Our Lives* while placidly knitting. She asked me how school had been, and I told her that it had been okay. She then told me that she suspected that Lennie Summock was around the corner with his ex-girlfriend, and if he thought for one minute that she was to be taken for a fool, his whorish ass had another thing coming.

"Ma, what makes you think that?"

"Tracy, don't be so naive. That is all he does."

"Well, Ma, you told me that y'all were just friends, so why you so uptight about his doings?"

"That's besides the point. He has been coming around pretending that he didn't have nobody, when I knew all along that he was still around that corner. If he comes out there, he is not getting in. You better not say a word!"

After weighing the conversation, I suddenly announced, "Ma, I'm going on a date."Neeyla then stopped short of any further conversation about Lennie, and gave me a blank stare. After a while, Neeyla poised her mouth, and I was sure the cursing was about to erupt. To my surprise, she didn't say anything but "Who is he?"

I very innocently added, "The boy who put my scholarship in the newspaper, Raymir Gorman."

Neeyla cocked her eyes and said, "I thought that guy was way older than you, and already out of college. You don't need to be dating nobody like that, who's already out of college."

CHAPTER 15

# RUST COLLEGE

That summer I learned painful lessons about loving and living. It was the summer of 1987, and I was slowly coming of age.

After a long fought battle of independence from Neeyla, I packed a small suitcase and stayed with Carrie for two weeks. It all started when I told her that I should have a boyfriend before I went to college, so I left home early one morning with Raymir Gorman, and did not return until evening. Neeyla thought I was off doing the nasty with that boy, but in truth, I was helping his mom clean out some closets. When I returned home that evening, Neeyla tanned my hide black and blue. After this, Grandma told her that I was a young adult, and that she needed to respect that. By the time school rolled around, I had returned home with Neeyla, finally accepting the fact that I was a young adult about to go off to college.

The trip to Holly Springs was a reverie of snarled kudzu all the way down Highway 7 to I-55 North. Rust College sat quietly cornered in a square section of town as soft breezes gently kissed tall summer grass. As we rode through the downtown section, we witnessed the buzzing of shoppers who were more than eager to trade their earnest earnings for newfound goods. The face of the town still wore the expression of an aged, old southern relic cast beneath the exterior of quaint antique stores. Little elderly ladies in pearl earrings with matching shoes, pocketbooks, and summer sweaters peered from behind glasses at well-worn receipts. Miserly men who had not seen the sun in weeks marched mechanically behind their brides of youth, inquisitively inspecting all that was in sight.

As we drove through the center of town, Lennie Summock, Neeyla, and I witnessed that Holly Springs was yet another piece of Mississippi's iconic history, with its share of mid-wives tales and quaint customs. As with most rural southern towns, the town matched the people, and the people matched the town, as they so appeared. Rust College was founded in 1866 by the Freedman's Society and the United Methodist Church with the purpose of educating emancipated slaves.

The sun greeted me in blindfolds that day as we made our way to the admissions and financial aid offices. Lines of parents and students were sprawled, and redoubled from the financial aid offices way down into the hallway. After standing for a good while, the crowd dispersed and reassembled in alphabetized sections in accordance with last names. Finally, Rust College had become my reality. After registration was completed, and my full scholarship was in tow, we were directed by student body members to our dormitories.

Trudging my way back up the stairway, I was accosted by a group of giddy freshmen who looked like real-life Barbie fashion plates. The all wore denim jackets, blaring bright pink lipstick, with matching nails and toenails.

The shortest girl in the group made herself known as Muffin. Muffin had a sweet air of cordiality about her. She dawned a pageboy haircut and matching dimples. "Hi, I'm from Denver, Colorado. Where are you from? And what's your name?"

"My name is Tracy Lynn, and I'm from Greenwood, Mississippi."

"I'm Muffin, and these are my friends from Kenya, Bay Saint Louis, and Water Valley, Mississippi."

"Hi," they all motioned.

"Nice meeting y'all, and hope to see you around," I said, as I glided slowly past them while one girl, Pantemonea, in the group mean-mugged me with heavily painted dark eyes."Tracy Lynn," said Muffin, "meet us in the lounge at five o'clock so that we can all walk to the courtyard for the step show at six this evening."

As we walked to my dorm room, I thought to myself that this was going to be my home for the next nine months, so I may as well make the most of it. Inside, the dorm smelled of fresh linen and country pine, with a slight coating of summer dust. Lennie strategically placed my trunk in the closet, while Neeyla placed the remaining bags on the floor next to my bed. They both sat down for a while from sheer exhaustion, and gave me the real on life. Lennie told me to stay away from knuckleheads, and Neeyla told me to take my pills every day. After a while, it was time for them to go, and I said momentary goodbyes to Lennie and Neeyla as I walked them back downstairs, and then watched them as they drove way out of sight. All of a sudden, I found myself in a world that was different from any I had known. When I couldn't see their car in sight anymore, I bounded back up the stairs in high hopes of a bright future.

By the time I approached my dorm room, I heard loud noises coming from inside, and gathered that my roommate had made it in. Assembled inside the room were two girls who appeared to be sisters, standing next to their parents. As I entered the room, they momentarily paused to greet me.

"Hi, we are the Tony family from Macon, Georgia, and these are our daughters, Verancia and Yameldia. Verancia will be your roommate."

Simultaneously, both girls and I uttered a high pitched "Hi" in unison.

I could tell that Verancia's family was pretty rich. She had Louis Vuitton luggage for days, a big television, and a closet full of dresses and skirts in every shade of pastel that you could imagine. I smiled a sincere smile, and walked to my side of the room and continued to unpack my things. After a while, Verancia's mom motioned a wave at me as the family took the conversation out in the hallway to tell their children goodbye until the next time.

*This girl's family is rich, for sure,* I said to myself as I pensively stared at the huge suitcases on the floor.

Meanwhile outside in the lobby, suitcases rolled and rumbled well into the evening as parents and their college students parted ways. After putting the finishing touches on my side of the dormitory, and deciding that it was the best that it was going to get, I decided to re-acquaint myself with Muffin and her friends. The outside lobby was swarming with college students as high-pitched sounds of mirth encircled the room. Looking for familiar faces, I saw Muffin's hand wave at me from a far side of the lobby. As usual, her entourage was fully encircled around her, only this time, they had all changed into short shorts with matching crop tops.

As I got closer, I stated, "Why didn't somebody send me the memo?"

They all shook with laughter as they touched my hair, wanting to know if it was real. My eyes widened in amusement as they told me that it looked like tracks in my hair. I then propelled my hair forward, letting all of my hair fall to the front of my face, and then quickly bounced it back to mid-waist.

"Girlfriends, ain't no tracks here, and besides, Neeyla don't allow no stuff like that."They all asked, "Who is Neeyla?"

I told them that Neeyla was my momma in Greenwood, Mississippi. They thought that was funny too. Amelia, the one from Kenya, touched my hair and told me that I must be mixed to have hair like that.

Soon the courtyard became emblazoned and brightened with guys in white sport coats twirling fancy candy canes. Those boys were so fine and pretty, twirling them candy canes high up in the air with the tips of their fingers, and then twirling them back down real low. I just stood there and stared with my mouth wide open, because I had never seen no boys that fine before. I must have gone into a trance, because the next thing I knew, Muffin was pulling my arm and telling me to look at a group of girls in lovely soft pink skirts with matching parasols who were coming up from behind the trees, singing. As they danced to the forefront, they uttered a high-pitched call in unison that I had never heard before. Soon, girls in dazzling reds and flashing blues came in behind them, each with a style of their own. We all stood in the cool of the evening, engaging with the Greeks and watching the show until it was time to go back in.

Classes began on Monday, and carried long assignments well into the night. I became well acclimated with campus life, weekly research reports, and assembly programs. The weeks spun by like the threads in a sewing machine, and the wind was growing colder as the days, weeks, and months advanced upon themselves. I would call home to Neeyla on most Fridays and Saturdays when I couldn't get a ride home. During one of our conversations, she told me that she and Lennie Summock had finally called it quits when she found out that he was cheating with a woman around the corner who was older than she was. Neeyla said that she thought it was a sanctified woman who wasn't satisfied, from his church. Of course, I never mentioned it to Neeyla, but Lennie had brought his girlfriend on two occasions when he'd come to pick up his sister, Sandra, and me on the weekend. Since I didn't want Neeyla to be upset, I kept it to myself, all the while thinking about the games people play.

CHAPTER 16

# CHRISTMAS HOLIDAYS

By the end of the first semester, I had garnered a 3.5 GPA, and was well acclimated into the ways of college life.

Friday came with swift feet, and it was only a few days before I would return home for the Christmas holidays. This week, the assembly program was held on Friday, and I found myself in a reverie of deep thoughts as the speaker walked to the platform. Words permeated the atmosphere, spoke volumes, and became silent tombs as the audience waned in total restlessness. Then suddenly, a mighty choir with the voices of angels rushed to the stage in blue robes, and brought the life back into the room as they sang "Elijah Rock." Just sitting there watching that a cappella choir made my heart leap for joy. Grandma Carrie had told me many years before, she wanted me to attend Rust College, since we would watch the morning show together, and the a capella choir would sing at the end. So far, I'd held fast to my promise. Just as I was reminiscing in a journey of thoughts, a tall bass alto singer with a brass voice erupted from the crowd, singing his heart out, when all of a sudden some of the foolish freshman thought his facial expressions were some show for the light of heart. I personally thought it was just pure ignorance to laugh at that guy like that in his face, even though he was making some strange-looking faces as he sang. I was just glad that Neeyla had taught me to give respect to whom respect was due, but this Generation X sometimes, I just wondered.

That evening, I rode home with Raymir Gormon, and he thought it his business to keep on asking me if I was a virgin.

"Mmm, hmm, when you gon' let me hit that? Has anybody got that yet?" he intoned while singing along with New Edition's "Tenderoni."

I turned around from staring straight ahead, and asked him, "Have you lost your damn mind? And just because you're giving me a ride, doesn't mean I'm going to give you some coochie."

"Lighten up, baby, you ain't got to get all mad about it. Dang, girl! You coming out on me like the Black ninja. Jeez!"

"Well, stop asking me, because it won't do you no good, so you may as well not even ask."

Afterwards, we were just silent for a long time while he sat over there making funny faces. He played a few more old school songs, and with his usual dose of antics, reached out and slapped the top of my breast, so I slapped his hand back in return. Laughter erupted and drove out all the anger.

"Baby, lighten up," he said again. "You're so foxy, but you act like a little stiff old lady. Girl, you better learn to let your hair down and shake yo booty, because life is for the living."

He seemed to be the most carefree guy I'd ever known. Yet on his sad days, you just wanted to reach out and hug him, because it seemed as if his whole world were crashing down.

The sun followed us back to Greenwood, and I leaped out of the car in delight when I reached my grandmother's house. They were all seated around the front porch, and started putting their hands over their mouths, making "ooh wee" sounds, saying, "Tracy's got a boyfriend."

I walked past them shaking my head, saying, "He's not my boyfriend. He's just my friend."

The younger ones, along with Eloise and Luella, started singing, "But she says he just a friend."

I quickly went in the house, letting the screen door slam behind me.

Neeyla then said, "Tell that boy to get out of that car so I can get another real good look at him."

Raymir burst out of the car like he was some type of Hulk Hogan. The entire porch shook with laughter as he skipped across the porch making faces.

My grandmother introduced herself, and Alvin proudly reached out his hand and said, "Pleased to meet you."

Neeyla looked at him and said, "Don't be feeling on my daughter."

"Yes, ma'am, I wouldn't dare dream of it," he lied. Raymir was smiling a smile just as big as all out doors as he carried my suitcase in through Eloise's bedroom.

From that moment on, Raymir and I were a hit, as far as they were concerned. In fact, every time I came home from college, they would all ask, "Where is Raymir?" if they didn't see him. Carrie offered him a big plate of summer greens, along with buffalo fish, mashed potatoes, and hush puppies, which he proudly took.

"Girl, you done put your whole foot in this," he declared. "And I'm gon' eat 'em with my fingers like my momma taught me."

Granny just laughed and gave him a big ole bear hug while handing him the plate, for she lived by the motto, "If I cook it, then I want you to eat it." I then followed Grandma Carrie back into the kitchen, where she was already preparing sweet potato pies and homemade cakes, since Christmas would be the following Monday. Savory allspice and nutmeg rested heavily in the atmosphere, both intoxicating and mesmerizing the senses. After all those years, Alvin and Carrie were still giving each other the eye, and when their eyes met from across the room, you could still see the fire in them. Carrie's fast self still had it, and the thrill wasn't gone nowhere.

As for now, Alvin would sit quietly in the den in quiet corners, watching his favorite *Soul Train* reruns, while Carrie was in the kitchen measuring out just the right amount of this and that for her prized streusel swirl cake made from scratch. "Hey, Flipadiddy, come and give Granny some sugar," she said with a big smile."Hey, Grandma, what you been doing?"

"This old lady is trying to hold it together and keep our heads above water. It ain't always easy, with all these grown folks round here trying to take over my house, and not being grateful and appreciative of what they have. It just don't make no kind of sense."

"I do understand, Grandma," I assured her.

I already knew that with Neeyla back home, she was most likely the ringleader of it, since she was always in Carrie's and Alvin's business, sticking her nose in places it shouldn't have been and making smart comments, at that. Many times, I'd told Momma to mind her own business, and she just told me to get me some business like I was the one starting stuff. Like Reena said, "Neeyla needs to get a grip instead of sitting around all the time, whining and complaining about ole possum-face Miquel, when he probably on top of somebody right now, even as we speak." Reena said she wouldn't let no grass grow under her feet for nobody, and they wouldn't know which door she went in or came out of. I tell you, Reena sure wasn't going to let any grass grow under her feet, and I loved Aunt Reena to the core, along with the good and bad.

"Flipadiddy, pass me those eggs and get me a stick of margarine out of the refrigerator."

I was basking in and relishing the moment, for I had my Grandma to myself, just as I had many years before when she'd first taught me to drink coffee.

I asked her if she remembered those days, and she said, "How could I ever forget them? It was when Jab and I had separated, not long after we were displaced by the tornado. My six children and I were living in separate places for a while, and I didn't know what I was going to do, but God made a way out of no way. We didn't have food, clothes, or anything. It was not until I started working for the Buergermots that I began to see my way. Mrs. Buergermot gave us clothes, and made sure that we had a tab at Sammy's so that we didn't want for anything. We came up from a hard way, but God always puts miracles in plain view right in front of our face so that we know beyond the shadow of a doubt that it was Him, and not us ourselves. Some folks declare that God ain't performing miracles, and that was the God of the Bible days. But I, for one, can tell you that God is the same God yesterday, today, and forever. He is still in the miracle-working business, and I'm a living witness that He is still performing miracles. Sometimes my way gets hard, and this ole lady knows that one day she will lie down on her cooling board."

"Ah, Grandma, don't talk like that!"

"Flipadiddy, I've been around for a long time; all of my children are grown, and you my first grandbaby. Now you even grown, so I guess my work here is done."

"Granny, you talking like that 'cause you're upset, and rightfully so. Yet you got a lot of living left on the outside and the inside. Grandma, you have no wrinkles, and still have your Coca-Cola bottle shape. I just pray that I'm half as fine as you when I'm your age."Granny's smile infused the entire room. She offered me a piece of leftover buffalo fish from lunch, which I eagerly ate with greedy lips. Fried fish was always a weekend staple at her house, and when we were younger, Granny would only let us eat buffalo because the brim and perch fish had too many bones in it. She was smiling again, and that was all that mattered.

Alvin managed to leave his seat and join the merriment in the kitchen. He hugged my shoulder and told me that he was proud of me. "Y'all already out of school," he said. "Yo momma couldn't wait to see you. You all she's been talking about. What you taking up in school?"

"English, education, and journalism," I told him.

"All right, make Momma proud, and stay out of trouble." "By the way, y'all, Reena wrote me and told me she wants me to go back to study abroad in Africa with her family this summer."

Before I scarcely got the words out of my mouth, Grandma Carrie was screaming, "Neeyla, come here and listen to what your daughter is saying!"

Neeyla was in the kitchen in the speed of light, breathing real hard. "What's wrong?" she said.

"Flipadiddy, repeat what you just said."

When I looked around, I realized I had an audience, because the entire family had run into the kitchen.

"Ma, can I go to Africa with Aunt Reena?"

"Go where? I beg your pardon!"

"Aunt Reena wants me to go back to Africa with her this summer to help teach a class of natives."

"You tell Reena's hot ass to find her something to do, like spend that man's money."

"Ma, she said call her!"

"I ain't calling a damn thang! The last time I called her she didn't even bother to answer. You ain't going, and that's the final answer, with all them wild ass animals roaming around everywhere. If I didn't let you go to Florida with your own daddy, then you know good and well I'm not letting you go to no Africa."

"But Ma, I'm eighteen!"

"What's that supposed to mean?"

I decided not to say anything else, since she about to wage all-out war. Grandma then starte "Flipadiddy wants to go to Africa."

By that time, after all was said and done, the rated from the kitchen back into thin air. Grandma just looked at me and smiled, and told me that Neeyla would come around. Personally, I think Momma was still mad with Reena about some stuff that happened nearly twenty years ago out there on that Money Road. I decided to talk with my Aunt Luella about it when Neeyla was nowhere around.

If you ask me, I thought Dr. Reena Olujare was living a charmed life with her Nigerian husband in suburban Illinois. She was educated, made her own money, and had married money, coupled with good looks. Reena had met Adebiyi in undergraduate school at Illinois State, and brought him home one summer to meet Uncle Sammy and Big Momma. Big Momma asked him what was he gonedo with a fast-tail gal like that, and he replied, "Worship and adore her, for she is my queen." Big Momma laughed so loud that you could hear the echo all the way across the cotton fields. Adebiyi just stood there and smiled a great big sincere smile, acting like he had never had no girlfriend in his life.

Big Mama then said, "Boy, she must of gave you some of that poontang."

Adebiyi smiled with a look of disbelief on his face. "Big Mommare," he said, "what is poontang?" in a very heavy Nigerian accent.

Big Momma looked at him, grinning, and made the nasty symbol with her hands and said, "Poontang," making her voice sound African too.

"Ohh, I see! Poontang. Ohh." Adebiyi laughed. "You see, in my country, we are not allowed to consummate our marriage until after the marriage vows and the wedding."

"Boy, talk plain English so I can understand what you mean."

t means that we do not sleep together until after the wedding day."

Big Momma laughed again. "Well, you should have met fast tail when she was twelve or thirteen. That's how Neelya got that baby at fourteen; they running to clubs at night, showing they business, and laying up on the river bank with them fast-talkin' niggas till one of 'em got pregnant. Should have known Reena was too hot to get one. Neeyla, however, was just the right speed to catch a baby. Slow!"

Uncle Sammy said, "Momma, that's enough," and grabbed Adebiyi's shoulder and asked him if he wanted to go fishing later that evening, and not to listen to Big Momma's stories.

When Neeyla got married, of course, Big Momma had already gone home to be with the Lord. I bet she's still on the other side laughing out loud. Of course, Neeyla told her, "That dude was funny looking, with them big white teeth," but said he worshiped the ground that Reena walked on, although they broke up for a season when Reena said that she needed to take a break from dating. However, Adebiyi made a solemn vow that Reena was his queen, and that the crown had become two. Imagine that! No matter what Reena did, he promised to be there waiting for her. Uncle Sammy had previously told Neeyla that she was going to get just what she was looking for, foolin' with all them different types of guys. Then, without notice, right before Reena graduated from college, she announced that she was thinking about getting married. The next thing we knew, she and Adebiyi were married. I guess Miss Reena finally got tired of all her little rendezvous games.

At any rate, Reena had a Benz when very few of us even had cars. She lived in a very opulent neighborhood comprised of white, predominately white, and Jewish neighbors. The house was so big that it had its own swimming pool and outdoor kitchen. Reena's husband Adebiyi was a practicing optometrist with the state of Illinois, and had a thriving clinic on the lower Southside of Chicago. Reena taught English literature and African American studies at the University of Illinois.

Momma said that when Reena got with that man and married him, she got beside herself, snubbing her nose down on the family and calling them "country." From what I could tell, Reena was not snobbish at all. She was just the same as she'd always been. Reena only wanted a better way of life for herself, as well as her family.

Poe, Reena's twin brother, could write a book on that. Lord knows Reena spent some money bailing him out of trouble. Poe made an entire career of being in and out of jail since the train accident with Johnny Boy. Some people just never learn. Reena bought him a car, set him up in a nice apartment, and tried to get him to go to back to school, but to no avail. She was practically raising his oldest daughter Amiracle with him being in and out of jail. Amiracle's mom overdosed on pills when Amiracle was four, and she'd been with Reena ever since, because Poe just couldn't seem to get his act together.

CHAPTER 17

# CHRISTMAS DAY SERVICE

Sunday came, and the next day would be Christmas Day.

Eloise and I, along with Davis, decided to attend Sunday morning service at Elder Layman's church down the street at the corner of Dewey. We were all up and dressed by ten in preparation for Sunday school and the eleven o'clock morning worship service. We ascended the church steps fully clad in new Christmas outfits. Sunday school was still in session, so we decided to sit at the back of the church as to not be so obvious.

When we sat down, a thin, tall solemn looking usher motioned us to move to the middle of the sanctuary. Eloise gritted her teeth and said, "Ma'am, I don't wish to sit at the front of no church. I'm fine just where I am." I elbowed Aunt Eloise, who was gaining an audience as some of the adult Sunday school members had turned around and started staring at us. We finally settled back down in our seats, and by that time, Eloise was staring back at them, rolling her eyes and wondering what they were staring at. I did my best to distract Eloise Gaye by diverting her attention to the visitor's packet, which the ushers had given us to complete.

The pastor of the church mounted the platform as the entire congregation began to sing "I Got the Victory." Pastor Layman led the song in an upbeat tempo of praise and worship, which made you just want to jump up and stump your feet. The entire congregation was shouting and dancing the victory dance, when suddenly a woman with a brightly-colored suit and matching hat started to dance out from the congregation, skipping to the rhythm of the beat. Praises overflowed with an array of hallelujahs as Pastor Layman began to shout.Eloise and Mason thought the woman's dancing was funny, and Eloise started laughing out loud. I whispered in her ear and told her that God didn't like ugly, but she kept on smiling. Pastor Layman, a small-framed man with a deep alto voice, who appeared to be relatively youthful, was a native of California, and had moved to the Delta to answer God's call. He preached a very lively message on the Savior's birth, on "Being Born Without.""Jesus, Mary's baby was born in a stable because there was no room in the inn.Jesus will bring you out to bring you in." Pastor's Layman's words flowed into the congregation with fervency and power.

At the end of service, he asked all visitors to stand and give the names of their church homes. We all stood, and I told them our names, and that I was a member of Wesley United Methodist Church; that Eloise and Davis were my aunt and youngest uncle. Pastor Layman told us that he was glad that we had chosen to worship with them and to come again. As we went back out of the church, we were greeted by cousins and kin people who were members of Living Faith. They hugged and kissed us, telling us how much we had grown, and asked about the rest of the family. We reciprocated the hugsand marched back down the seat to Carrie's house.

As we got closer to the house, we noticed some extra cars parked in the driveway with out-of-state license plates. Then I saw a shiny black Benz with Illinois license plates and felt my heart race with excitement. Aunt Reena was in town, and it was about to be on. I ran the rest of the way, all the way up the steps, and bounded through the front door. Not seeing anyone but Reena, I ran past the family gathered in the front room and jumped right into Reena's arms.

She screamed, "Tracy Lynn!" She hugged my neck real tight, saying, "Girl, you're even prettier than the pictures. Girl, you yo momma's twin all over again. Neeyla, this girl look like you spit her out. Roscoe ain't had none in this act."

"Aunt Reena, I'm so glad you're here!"

"Tracy Lynn, how you been darling?" she said, all the while hugging me tighter.

Reena looked like she had stepped out of the pages of *Ebony* magazine. Reena was real fine too. Her high, ruddy-colored cheekbones sat snugly amidst a serenade of smiles. Reena had a strong country dialect, and was just as country as she could be, only real proper with it, pronouncing every syllable yet country at the same time. Her sense of style was every woman's heart's desire. She was wearing a snug-fitting winter white skirt set with matching pumps. Each drape of fabric caressed her skin like a pair of silk stockings. And when she moved, it seemed both time and space stood still just to inhale her essence.

I hugged Reena again, saying, "Aunt Reena, I'm so glad you're here."

"Tracy Lynn, do you remember my brother Poe? Well, Poe is incarcerated, but I brought someone with me. Tracy Lynn, meet your cousin, Amiracle. Amiracle, meet Tracy Lynn."

Amiracle looked just like Aunt Reena, only she had golden hair and hazel green eyes.

"Hey," she said tersely after hugging me and shuffling back to her seat. "Family, as you know, Adebiyia is from Nigeria, and we're going home to spend the summer in Nigeria. There are so many places in the villages that have been decimated by poverty and poor nutrition. Adebiyia is taking his healing back to the homeland. Neeyla Jean, you gotta let her go so she can learn about her ancestry. Besides, she's so talented, and can offer so much to the children of the village. Let your daughter experience life and living. On top of that, you need to go your own self. Girl, Momma used to be as fine as wine when she was courting your daddy." Then Reena started laughing with that big ole high-pitched laugh.

As she was about to turn back the pages of time, Carrie yelled loudly from the kitchen, "Come and get it!"

We all made a mad dash to the kitchen. Rena sat curtly at the far end of the table next to Carrie as Adebiyia pulled Reena's chair out for her and offered Neeyla a seat as well. Instead, Neeyla yanked back her seat with a scowl on her face, causing Eloise to burst out in an explosion of laughter. Adebiyia smiled delightfully as he waited for the family to be seated. Carrie laid a wide pan of cornbread dressing and sweet rolls on the table. Alvin pulled a golden-brown roasted hen and pineapple-glazed ham from the oven. Turnip greens and pork chitterlings were passed around to waiting plates. Adebiyi announced that he would gladly carve the hen, since his hobby as a boy had been emulating the Obaian images of the ancestral kings.

Adebiyi carved both the hen and the ham with the delicacy of a skilled artisan. "Mama Kayree, when I was a young child in my native land, my father taught me to carve in the old way of the Yoruba. My grandmother, being Igbo, married a man of the Yoruba tribe. My family helped pay my college tuition for medical school through the work of their hands. We were village craftsmen and tribesmen skilled in the way of our ancestors. Nothing came for free. Long hours we spent working each day, cutting wood and carving masks and statues for trading in the neighboring village. Each night, after a long day of cutting and carving wood, I would study by my bedside so that I could earn a high mark on my college admittance exam for a scholarship.

"You see, my grandmother and other members of my kinsmen suffered from poor vision because of diet. When I was quite young, I made a vow to my grandmother that I would one day bring medicine back to the village for the healing of eyes. When she passed away, she was totally blind. This moved my heart greatly because my grandmother's light had gone out of her temple. Each night, as I studied quietly by my bedside, I would hear my grandmother pray to God in her native Igbo tongue. She would thank God for the beautiful blessings of life, and all that God had done in her family's life. She would cry out from her heart to God that there would always be provisions of food and shelter for her family. In closing her prayer, she would always ask God to instill the gift of healing in my hands. As long as I live, I shall never forget my grandmother's prayers. It is because of her that I am, who I am, Adebiyi Olujare, the son of Yoruban kings, for 'Olujare' means 'God wins. His glory, He will not give to another.'"

I started to clap as Alvin, Luella, and Eloise chimed in. Adebiyi's eyes welled with tears, and Reena met him in a warm embrace. **Unspeakable joy walked in that day from the distant native shores of Africa. We had become one.**

After we had all eaten way past the full capacity, Carrie uncovered a dark chocolate fudge cake, her specialty, a streusel swirl, and a lemon pound cake, along with some sweet potato pies.

"Ooh, Momma Carrie! I'm 'bout to bust out of this skirt if I eat another bite," declared Reena.

Alvin then agreed that he couldn't eat another bite either. The table slowly started emptying itself, leaving only Reena, Neeyla, me, and Carrie.

"Reena, how long are you going to be here?" I asked.

"We will be staying with relatives in Itta Bena until New Year's, and then we're headed back to Chicago. I have to go back to work, and Adebiyi has to return to his practice.""Well, when y'all going back to Africa?"

"When school's out in early June, we will fly to Nigeria. Adebiyi has practitioners in his clinic who can see patients while he is away."

"Reena, you were always so intelligent, and carried yourself well. I'm proud of you."

"Thank you, Momma Carrie. I wouldn't trade you for the world."

"Neeyla Jean, how you feeling? You awfully quiet over there. You must be thinking about your bae. Where is he? Y'all still," insisted Reena.

"Baby, that possum face is back in St. Louis."

"Y'all separated. Well, as the song goes, if it don't fit, don't force it."

"Now you talking. That wouldn't 'bout it. I let that go four years ago," said Neeyla."Girl, get you a divorce, get your fine back, and get you a boo thang."

"I'm not thinking about no boo thang. Get you some business."

"I have some—yours.""Reena, what did you say?"

"I said you need to get yourself together. You sitting in this house, letting the whole world pass you by, pining after a Negro who done had mo' tail than the law allows. Neeyla, I never cared for him after the day he jumped you on the lake. I wanted to come and get y'all then, but you wouldn't have it. Neeyla, look at you, you don't even look like yourself with all of this weight on you. Are you trying to kill yourself? Neeyla, there are still some good men left, and my marriage is certainly not without its share of troubles. However, Adebiyi and I have vowed to love each other through it all. I miss my cousin. Where is she, Neeyla? Don't destroy your life. Sometimes we love and we lose."

"Reena, you never had that problem."

"Hold up, Neeyla! Wait one minute. Do you know how many times I was done wrong by guys who I loved because I thought they loved me? Y'all thought I was just Fast-tail Reena, but I was looking for love in all the wrong places. Each new guy brought the same tale of woe-is-me, because I kept doing the same thing over and over, thinking each time would be different. The only thing that could become different was me. Until I changed, nothing else would. Adebiyi was the only man who truly loved me for who I am. We never slept together until we were married because it went against his customs. He told me if I became pregnant, we would already be married. I broke up with him not long after bringing him home while we were in college because I was used to being intimate with my boyfriend, and thought he had a problem. Well, he never left my side, and here we are, fifteen years later. He is my king, and I am his queen. Neeyla, Adebiyi taught me how to love myself through the eyes of God. God has so much for you and Tracy Lynn. Please consider my request. You know you're always welcome to come. Yes, we gon' get that fine back, and find you a Mandingo warrior."

They both laughed and laughed until Carrie told them they could help her and Eloise put away the food, or exit.

"Adebiyi, let's say goodnight."

"Mommare Kayree, it was my pleasure, and do come to my home to visit with Alvin. Goodnight." He kissed her on the cheek, and they left in the quiet of the night.

CHAPTER 18

# LAGOS STATE, NIGERIA

The beginning of June lit a fire way down deep in my soul, a burning fire that my soul could not hold.

Sleep had evaded both my mind and soul the night before. School had been out for over a month, and I was beaming with excitement, since in the wee hours of the morning, I would leave with Reena and Adebiyi for Lagos State, Nigeria. Neeyla had given me an entire list of dos and don'ts for when I got there, so I knew very well not to engage myself in any conversation with the natives.

Both Reena and Adebiyi arrived at four in the morning. Night had not yet traded its midnight persuasion for its fairer twin, and thus thick night clouds tightly embraced and hovered around the dark sky. With a quick knock on the front door, they quickly scurried up the front steps.

Reena's eyes were wide and aglow as she serenaded the living room, bringing an explosion of life into the dimly lit room.

"Neeyla Jean, rise and shine, for your Nigeria has come. I'm about to take your baby back with me for a little while," she exclaimed. "Ahh, cheer up, honey. She's only going to be gone for the summer."

"Reena, how could I possibly sleep at a time like this?" exclaimed Neeyla. "You have to know that this is not easy for me, letting my baby go across the world. Reena, y'all take care of my baby; she's all I've got."

"Don't worry, Neeyla. You can bet my life on it that Tracy Lynn will be taken care of. Remember, eighteen years ago, it was I who led you to James Roscoe himself on that far away Money Road. As far as I'm concerned, she's my baby too. Besides, Adebiyi has a nice home in the city that his sister lives in and takes care of for him. Adebiyi's sister is so excited about meeting Tracy. She will also have a calling card with a twenty-four-hour access so you can reach her anytime. Please trust and know that she is in good hands, but above all, she is in God's hands."

Adebiyi carried my luggage as Reena hugged Neeyla and me real tight. I held my momma and assured her that I would call her every day. We drove off quickly in the dark of the night, and I looked back for as long as I could, watching Neeyla's silhouette until I couldn't see her standing in the dark anymore.

"Tracy Lynn, my dearest, my prayer has been answered!" exhorted Reena. "Chile, you are on the way to the land of your ancestors."

"Aunt Reena, is it true that people who live in the bush run around half naked, and there are wild animals roaming around everywhere?"

"Girl, I declare your momma has given you a full dose of it." Reena laughed loudly in her usual way. "While it's true that many families still live far out in the bush, Adebiyi's family primarily lives in the city, where you will be attending classes with me. As I mentioned earlier, you are going to assist me in teaching English as a second language to a class of fifth grade Yorubians who speak broken English. Don't worry, they're not running around naked. On the other hand, there are many wild animals in Africa, but the Wildlife Preservation Society maintains measures to keep the animals in their natural habitat, and out of the city. On top of that, unless you're really close to the outskirts of the city, you won't see them. Trust me, animals are just as afraid of you, as you are of them until you wander off into their territory."

"Yes, this is true," exclaimed Adebiyi. "The key to life in the bush is to avoid traveling at night without heavy artillery."

I was beginning to feel an inner tightness in my chest at the mention of wild animals. I then decided to drive out the inner fear by settling down into a deep slumber. About an hour later, Reena gently aroused me from my sleep, telling me that we had arrived at Mississippi International Airport. Adebiyi quickly explained that there was very little time before we would have to board our plane, and for the first time, I heard him mumble something in his native Yorubian tongue, to which Reena quickly assented and nodded. Whatever he said must have been serious, because Reena grabbed my shoulder and told me to walk faster. The airport held a mystery of intricate gates and terminals we had to quickly navigate our way through. After retrieving our boarding passes from the flight attendant's desk, we momentarily stood in line as we made our way to the airplane.

"Aunt Reena, are you ever afraid when you fly?"

"Honestly, the first time, I thought I would pass out, since I've always been afraid of heights. The first time I actually flew was when I visited Adebiyi's family in Nigeria. There was inclement weather that day, and it really solidified my fears. Luckily our plane was delayed, so we ended up being rerouted, which essentially means that we went another way."All that school year, I had been saving up the excitement for my summer internship with Reena and Adebiyi, and I refused to be taken captive by any fears. Adebiyi sat near the window, and I sat snugly between them. He gave me a brief smile, and again, began momentarily conversing with Reena in that same language. I sat quietly nestled in with a look of both anticipation and consternation.

Reena, whose eyes were earnestly fixed on my expression while conversing with Adebiyi, said, "Don't worry, you will be fine." Adebiyi then patted my shoulder and smiled at me.

Through the tiny window, I was starting to see the tops of the trees and roofs of homes and businesses. From the sky's distance, the town turned into a deep green motley maze with veins of water scattered throughout. After a while, the clouds turned into white puffs, and so I decided to nap until the next stop.

CHAPTER 19

# DR. ADEBIYI OLUJARE

When I stepped off the plane with Reena and Adebiyi, my heart went on a personal journey and wrapped itself in the clover of my childhood as an interlude of drums beat within my soul.

It was late afternoon, and the sun shone brightly, hanging high in its native sky. A canopy of mountainous terrain enriched the deep rich sands of the sub-Saharan climate. Beautiful tropical flowers and lush trees adorned and intoxicated the atmosphere with fragrant perfume. A quick flashback transitioned my mind to the beautiful field of daisies Neeyla and I had often encountered on our many walks to downtown Greenwood. Now I was suddenly thousands of miles from the country that had given birth to my entire generation to a land that was an innate and ancestral part of my being. Upon waking this time, we exited the airport and were ushered into another black Mercedes, which looked exactly like the one I had seen during Christmas at Grandma Carrie's house. The driver, a tall, slim man in his fifties, had a marked decorum of cordiality about him. He greeted us in English with the same heavy accent as Adebiyi, and carried our bags to the car.

"Thanks so much, Amir," Reena said to him.

Adebiyi kissed Reena, got into another car with a waiting driver, and said that he would be home after work. I learned Amir was Reena's personal driver.

As we drove through the town of Ile-Ife en route to Lagos, Amir began to relate Yorubian tales of far and near, singing, "Great Ife! Great I love you. There's no other great in the universe. Another great Ife is counterfeit. Great! Great! Great! G-r-e-a-t!" He merrily sang the songs of his ancestors while jauntily driving along the winding gray roads.

"Reena, is this the same girl from the white lands that you told me about?"

"Amir, it's not white lands, but America."

"Reena, that is exactly what I'm talking about. Young lady, I have heard a lot about you. It is my good pleasure to meet you. Welcome to Ile-Ife, Osun State, the great city of love. I am Amir Abiola Ibidun because I was born during the first days."

I wanted to ask Amir what he meant by them the "first days," but I had been taught all my life that it was best to be asked up than asked back, so I decided not to invite myself to no questions, because at home you might get your face slapped for doing such.

In the midst of his singing, Amir suddenly uttered, "By the way, Reena, you have a letter from Poe, and a small package that I entrusted to Fatima." Fatima was Adebiyi's oldest sister who, being a widow, decided to care for the affairs and estate of her younger brother Adebiyi. "Tracy Lynn, Fatima has taken special care to ensure that the house is especially ready for your summer's stay."

After we had driven for a while, my favor suddenly shifted on a group of women and three teenage girls who were carrying their wares of brightly covered terra cotta on their heads. All were adorned with varying shades of brightly colored fabric, with matching head wear that accentuated their ebony skin, casting a black porcelain glow on their faces. The sunny shades of the fabric draped their bodies in such a way that their hips swayed in unison with each step.

Amir drove slowly while yelling from the window, "Hey, foxy momma, are you going to invite me over for dinner?"

The woman made a face and said, "Do I know you, dirty old man?"

"Well, I would like to get to know you."

She paused with her hands on her hips, saying, "What is your name, sir?"

"Amir, foxy momma," he said."

Then one of the girls shouted, "Dad, you got Mom blushing again!"

We all laughed as Amir slowly drove off, saying, "I will meet you in the evening before the sun goes down, and do wear my favorite perfume."

Reena laughed real loud again and said, "Amir, if I didn't know that was your wife, I would swear that you are a player."

"Recognize the player, Reena. Recognize," said Amir in his strong voice.

They laughed some more until I, too, started laughing.

"Amir, tell me, when are you going to invite me over for supper?" Reena giddily laughed."

"Reena, are you forgetting? We prepare that entire meal for you, and then busy lady—you don't show up."

"Amir, you know that Abediyi was called to an emergency that same eve of our supper, and that it was not entirely proper to indulge in the delicacies of your family table without my family being present."

"This is also true. That is exactly why I stated, young lady, when the time is right, we will gather around the table. Reena, do bring Fatima and Tracy with you."

I realized in the car that it was Amir's family that we had passed along the way. In time, I learned that Amir's first wife and daughter were killed in a fire during hunting season many years ago. Amir, being Yorubi, had also taken a wife of the Igbo tribe, and was now the proud father of three daughters, with twins on the way.

As we continued the long drive from the airport, we traveled farther into town, until we approached Reena and Adebiyi's home. The two-story edifice towered above a massive iron gate. As we entered the parking garage, an energeticbut shame-faced youngman named Adawa opened the gate. He and Amir soon began conversing in the same familiar language that Adebiyi and Reena had engaged in at the airport. The home looked like a stately mansion from a distant past. Huge arched windows adorned the second level, and a huge copper-colored iron door sat squarely in the midst, giving it the appearance of a gothic castle. Large handcrafted urns upturned native shrubs and flowering plants that were juxtaposed against the front entry. We had scarcely entered the driveway when, out of nowhere, a statuesque woman wearing bright yellow and leafy green with matching headwear dashed from the front door, saying, "Ekabo"—or "Welcome home."

We then all got out of the car and walked towards her. Both Reena and Amir said "Ekule" in return as they walked towards Fatima.

"Well, hello there, young lady. I am Fatima, Adebiyi's oldest sister. We will be spending a lot of time together, so I hope that you like to eat, because I have prepared quite a feast especially for you."

In truth, deep down inside, I was so full of excitement about seeing the Africa of my dreams, the one on all the postcards, pictures, and letters from Reena, that food was the farthest thing from my mind. Inside the home smelled of savory yams and fresh greens, which so reminded me of Grandma Carrie's kitchen in Greenwood. The entry room boasted exotic prints framed against rich ivory walls and sterling marble flooring. The furnishings were also made of embossed crocodile and zebra prints, with beautiful masks and ornamentation scattered throughout.

After walking through the entry room, we passed the dining room area, which housed a huge rectangular table made of rich cypress wood. On top of the table were three large hand-carved ebony bowls that complemented the rich brown coloring of the table. On the stove, stainless cooking pots stewed sumptuous smells throughout the house. As we walked through the large stately mansion, I was thinking to myself that I had never been inside a home that looked like this. Wow, not only did Aunt Reena have a lot of style, but she sure had a lot of taste too.

Fatima led me through a long corridor. "Tracy Lynn, girl, this is your room."

My heart was bursting with excitement as we walked into a huge ivory room with an ornately carved cypress headboard, where three large zebra-print pillows rested, in the same texture and print of a large storage ottoman seated at the foot of the bed. Hanging on the walls were oblong African prints that resembled the ones in the entry room, only they looked like abstract mazes. On the floor beneath the hangings were colorful African drums and carved figurines. My eyes became as big as marbles as I stared in awe at what was going to be my room for the next three months of summer.

Fatima opened a deep, long closet, and carefully laid my bags on the floor. "You can hang your things in here. There are some hangers and some ceremonial outfits for special occasions, and your uniforms for class. There are also books and magazines on both Yoruban and Ebo culture at the foot of your bed. Your own personal bathroom and toiletries are right here for you. Put your things down and come along, child." Fatima had long, silky lashes above a high-spirited smile. As friendly as she was, I could tell that she was not one to be reckoned with. Her graceful and toned form sacheted down the hall as the top of her skirt danced merrily upon her beautifully polished brass feet.

"Tracy, I'm glad you're here. You are so beautiful, and favor your kinsmen. Girl, you have apples in your cheeks like the women of Yoruba. Although many of our people were taken captive in strange ships, they are surely coming back to claim their ancestry."

Reena and Adebiyi's room was down the hall from Fatima's and mine. We passed a large, dimly lit study with elaborate furnishings and volumes of books. After traversing back through the kitchen, we walked to the other side of the house through a short hall. Fatima led me through the back of the house.

"Sometimes when we are tired of cooking inside, we come out here and cook the way our families and ancestors have been cooking for centuries."

More large cooking pots were lined up on empty shelves. There were also big pots on top of grills made from large gray stones. Fatima, in her heavy but proper accent, told me that the kitchen and combined garden was her favorite part of the house. "I like to come out here and pray to God almighty, and thank Him for always working in our lives. When I come out here, time just seems to stand still as I commune with Mother Nature. This is Fatima's garden. Indeed, it is my very own. I will show you. Over her, I grow fresh cassava, okra, garden eggs, spinach, and red peppers. In a little while, we will have fresh abacha, which is African salad grown from Fatima's garden. Let's say it slowly—ah-bah-cha."

Following Fatima's lead, I slowly pronounced it with her.

"Yes, darling, that is correct. Abacha. You will like it, and it is good for you."

We then walked farther back into the rear of the yard, where Fatima's entire garden was situated. Neat rows of manicured okra rose to meet the sun, trailing neighboring rows of bright, pungent red peppers. The rows of bright red peppers sent a familiar scent through my nostrils, and I laughed.

"Girl, why do you laugh?" questioned Fatima.

"It's not you, Fatima. My mother Neeyla loves cooking with peppers and hot spices. Her barbecue chicken is so hot and spicy that it makes you cry to eat it, but Fatima, it is so good."

"Yeah, girl, you are your kinsmen's daughter, for sure."

As we walked through the neat rows, we came upon a white vegetable that resembled green bell peppers.

"This here is a garden egg, which is another great ingredient for my delicious abacha.""Wow, Fatima, you have such a beautiful garden. It must require a great deal of work and patience to grow such a big garden."

"Young lady, patience is a virtue, and as I said before, time stands still when I come out here. Well, enough garden talk for one day, because we will come back out here often. When I am not inside, you will usually find me in my garden. Girl, let us go back inside, where it is cooler. You can go back to your room to wash for dinner, as I need to finish cooking it."

CHAPTER 20

# PREPARING FRESH ABACHA WITH FATIMA, MY BELOVED

Fatima veered back into the kitchen, and I pranced back down the hall into my bedroom and gently closed the door.

I couldn't wait to call Neeyla and tell her all about my trip. I dug deeply into the side pocket of my travel bag, and retrieved the calling card that Reena had given me. I quickly put in the code, followed by Neeyla's number.

"Hey, Momma's baby! You there? You done made it to the Motherland. Thank you, Jesus!"

"Yes, ma'am. Momma, I'm here. Momma, it's beautiful here, and Fatima, Adebiyi's sister, is so nice. And Momma, she has a big garden that is full of nice, delicious vegetables, like okra, rows of red peppers, and garden eggs that she grows herself, and uses in her cooking. I told her about your hot and spicy wings as well. She also thinks I resemble the people of Yoruba. Momma, this home is unreal, and unlike anything I've ever seen before. It has two stories with a huge iron gate around it, and a guard who lets us in and out. There are so many unique African furnishings and works of art. The entire house has white marble flooring. They even have a place out back to cook, where Fatima's garden is. On the way from the airport we drove past the outskirts of town, and I saw Reena's driver's family walking with wares on their heads. They are so pleasant and graceful. Tomorrow we are going downtown to Reena's classroom to prepare it for our students. Momma, I'm so excited, and love it here."

"You mean to tell me there is a gate around the house?! Just like I said, wild ass animals roaming around."

"No, Momma, Reena and Adebiyi live in town. They don't live in the bush."

"Stay inside that gate, because if I have to walk to Africa and get you, it's gon' be too bad for you and Miss Reena!"

"Momma, you don't have to worry about that. I only go out of the gate with Reena's driver in a car. We don't be walking anywhere."

"Good, and keep it that way. I think Miss Pat Ashley done got herself stuffed up again. She been going down there on that corner laying out with a straggly looking yellow tabby cat. Now she looks like who drug the cat out, stretched out asleep every day on the other side of the couch. I even put tape on her coochie to try to stop her from sleeping around with all of them rough-looking tomcats, but, well, I guess it didn't work." She laughed. "Pat Ashley and all them illegitimate chaps are going straight to the humane society. I'm not about to be bothered with a thousand cats. Pat Ashley is enough all by herself."

Pat Ashley was our bright calico cat of many colors. With me being away all summer, Neeyla seemed to be preoccupied with Pat Ashley's nightly wanderings. I could tell that she was trying to dispel the quietness in the house.

"I miss you, Momma."

"I miss you, too, baby."

"Momma, when I'm settled in, I will send you some pictures and a post card. Give Carrie and them my love. Well, I just wanted to call and tell you that I love you."

"I love you, too, baby."

After conversing with Neeyla, I decided to see what was in the trunk at the foot of the bed. I thumbed past numerous stacks of Yoruban magazines and found a book on the history of Yoruba. There were also a few illustrated books on African art and culture. At the bottom were forgotten family photos in a Ziploc bag. Reena and Adebiyi looked much younger. A gentle knock on the door reminded me that we would be eating in an hour, so I would save the photos for later. I quickly closed the ottoman and decided to freshen up, after which, I rejoined Fatima back in the kitchen.

The large cooking pots danced on the burners of the oven and spewed out aromatic spices. Fatima was busy preparing some softened white noodles. "Tracy Lynn, come join me so you can help prepare our evening meal. I'm going to show you how to prepare fresh abacha, African salad grown straight from the garden. Come," she motioned.

I eagerly stole quietly to stand next to Fatima.

"Girl, the secret to making abacha is to use only the best and freshest ingredients, which I grow right from my garden." Fatima lifted the lid from a large steaming pot. "This is palm oil and diced tomatoes, which have been slowly cooking. We are going to stir in the onions." She motioned for me to pass the onions. "You stir, while I prepare the potash, which is a meat tenderizer." Fatima pointed to me to add the mixture of ground ehu, crushed red peppers, stock cubes, crayfish, and upaka leaves. I carefully and nervously added each ingredient, making sure that the rich, red savory paste, which was turning golden, did not stick to the bottom of the pan.

"Wow, Fatima, it's turning yellow."

"Yes, that is the rich coloring of the abacha."

"Fatima, are those ramen noodles?"

"No, girl, this is finely grated cassava. It is made from a root called cassava which resembles yam. The ones growing in the garden are not yet ripe, but, my dear one, we will purchase some fresh cassava from the market, and I will show you how to both prepare and store it so that looks like your ramen noodles."

"Fatima, do I need to continue to stir?"

"No, girl, turn off the pot. You can slice the garden egg while I slice this large onion.""Fatima, it all smells so good."

"Yes, yes, you will like it. Meanwhile, we must add the final ingredients, diced pomo, which is cooked cow's skin. Finally, my dear, soaked and drained abacha into all the final ingredients."

Fatima pulled eight carved wooden bowls from the top shelf and instructed me to retrieve the three large black bowls from the dining room table. "We are going to serve our dinner in these large wooden vessels. Take this towel and rinse these bowls while I put the abacha into the salad bowls."

I quickly washed the large bowls, and went back to the island counter to help Fatima with the abacha. We scooped the abacha into the small bowls with large wooden ladles.

"Lastly, we are going to garnish with onion, garden eggs, and steamed fish."

Both Fatima and I went back and forth in the kitchen, laying the evening meal out until it was time to eat. Just as we were finishing, Reena and Adebiyi walked through the front door, bringing with them the noise and bustle of the city's business. Reena danced gleefully into the kitchen with Adebiyi's bright smile right behind hers, hugging and kissing both me and Fatima.

"Tracy Lynn, look at you, already in the kitchen, cooking our favorite meal. Ooh, Fatima, you didn't! Okra stew, palm nut stew, abacha, my absolute favorites. Girl, you and Tracy Lynn have outdone yourselves! This all looks so lovely. Adebiyi, let's go wash up for dinner."

In the meantime, I continued to assist Fatima in spreading out the delicious delicacies on the dining table. Before long, we had all sat down to enjoy the family meal. After Adebiyi said grace, Fatima played some upbeat African music with drum instrumentals, and Adebiyi started singing while Reena joined in. We all started laughing again.

"Aunt Reena, you're killing it."

Mirth and laughter gathered around the supper table as rhythmic beats made beautiful melodies.

"Honey, Amir desires our company at his home. You remember the last time his wife Adaeze and her sisters prepared our favorite meal, and we could not go because you were called to an emergency surgery? Amir has been so loyal to our family, and Adaeze will be delivering the twins soon, so we must go and take Tracy."

"Yes, my dear, we must go and keep company with them as they name their twins during the naming ceremony. Tracy Lynn, Amir's wife Adaeze is from Igbo-Ora, which happens to be called the twin capital of the world because of an unusually high rate of twin births."

"Uncle Adebiyi, where is Igbo-Ora?" I asked.

"It is fifty miles north of our city of Lagos. The Yoruba have a tradition of celebrating the birth of a child, and as in this case, twins. A special naming ceremony takes place, where all the elders are present as well, when the baby turns seven days old. This special ceremony will prepare the way for the child's birth into the world for protection against harm, and for blessings of good fortune."

"Amir said the other day that Adaeze will deliver at the end of July. She is already seven months," added Fatima.

Uncle Adebiyi pulled Reena close and said, "Reena, we will host our own naming ceremony soon."

Reena smiled. "Soon. Yes, very soon."

Fatima's eyes, in an instant, diffused anger with a quick glance away from Reena, and I sensed that there were things seething below the surface of their otherwise happy marriage."Reena, I want some nieces and nephews to help spoil before I'm sleeping in my grave. Besides, girl, you're not getting any younger."

Adebiyi quickly changed the sting of the subject by saying to me, "So tell me, Tracy Lynn, do you like African cuisine?"

Both Fatima and Reena watched eagerly, and waited with their mouths wide open in anticipation of my response. By this time, their hearts were merry with the spirits of the rich liquor of which they'd heartily indulged.

I smiled sheepishly, and said, "It's all so delicious, but I really like the abacha and okra stew. However, I don't know about this fufu. At home, we mainly cook cornbread with our main dishes. I'm sure I can get accustomed to it, though, but it tastes a little funny to me."Laughter erupted from the table like hot molten lava, and Adebiyi burst into an explosion of singing with the rhythm of the drum, as Fatima happily sang along with him. "Fufu and soup, fufu and soup, fufu and soup, with some okra on the side."

By this time, Aunt Reena was dancing her way up from the table as she began clearing the dishes. Fatima, whose expression was still half hardened, rose to assist, saying, "Reena, go and kiss your husband goodnight. Tracy and I will clean the kitchen."

Reena kissed me goodnight and walked gingerly behind Adebiyi.

"Besides, Lotus is coming this week to help clean and relieve me."

Lotus was the house assistant.

CHAPTER 21

# NIGHTTIME PHANTASMS

Sleep was restful, and embodied my inner being with phantasms of wild beasts and Benin kings in the battle over the great throne.

The great lion and his roaring pride marched in array against the bronze-clad king and his mighty bronze army. The pride of lions continued to advance forward with deafening roars and ominous snarls. Suddenly, the forest floor shook when the leader of the pride stood on his hind legs, and while beating his chest, declared, "I am the Great Calamari, the son of Calamari, the Fourth. Your heads will be feast for my kinsmen." However, the bronzes, who were covered in mail, all the while marched steadily without wincing or blinking against the Great Calamari. They marched in tempo, displaying ancient axes and shields as the flute players in the rear picked up the tempo. The mighty bronze king suddenly advanced forward with a procession of bronzes falling behind him, and launched a golden flaming ax, which severed the head of the Great Calamari. A mighty battle cry erupted from the bronzes as the head of the Great Calamari fell heavily through the forest floor. An explosion of bronzes pursued the fallen pride deep into the forest, where they reside until this day.

I woke up in a frightful sweat, grasping my pillow until my eyes re-adjusted, and I became reacquainted me with my surroundings. Streaks of silver moon climbed in through the solitary window and cast menacing forms on the whitewashed walls. The thud of the Great Calamari's head against the forest floor was still penetrating my thoughts with fear. I closed my eyes tightly in an attempt to reenter the safety of sleep, when suddenly thoughts of Grandma Carrie in her big comfy chair, with feet still in shuffle from a day's work, brought solace to my soul. She would sit way back in that chair in the middle of the night, telling us not to fear the dark, because the dead could not harm the living. Her warm and courageous spirit, all wrapped up in brown woolen socks, with well-worn house shoes, had a way of arresting one's soul into the deep slumber of night. Before long, the electric vibrating of my alarm clock was buzzing in my ears, ending the final comfort of my sleep.

Fatima's gentle knock on the door, along with her open entry, brought in the sweet smell of maple syrup and frying sausages. "Wake up, girl. Breakfast is almost ready."

Aunt Reena fell in right behind her, proclaiming in her usual upbeat voice, "Rise and shine, Tracy Lynn, this is the day that you meet your new students. Did you sleep well last night?"

With a half plastered-on smile, I said, "Aunt Reena, I've never slept so well. This bed feels good, and is fit for a queen." I decided not to tell Aunt Reena about my dream so she would not think that I was too afraid to carry out my assignment.

"I hope you like your room. Fatima and I put on the finishing touches just for you.""Aunt Reena, I really appreciate you taking the time to bring me here. Thanks for believing in me."

"Ah, darling, as I told your momma, from the moment you were conceived by James Lee Roscoe and Neeyla Jean, I vowed that you were just as much my child as hers, and watching you grow has been my greatest joy."

"Aunt Reena, where is Amiracle?"

"She is spending the summer in Chicago with her grandmother and younger siblings. I will be sending for her before summer's end so that you two can get to know each other, and witness the naming of Adaeze's twins." Aunt Reena slowly rose from the bed. Her thick black hair was falling loosely from its bun, gently grazing her shoulder. Aunt Reena was around thirty-five, the same age as Neeyla, but did not look a day over twenty-five. "Amir is coming around ten this morning, and orientation will begin at two o'clock. Oh, did you see your attire in the closet? The pupils wear uniforms, and you and I will both wear this." She sauntered to the closet and took out a brown and yellow skirt, with a matching top and head tie. "This top is called a buba, and the wraparound skirt is called an iro. Lastly, the head tie is called a gele. Get washed up for breakfast, and Fatima will help you get dressed afterwards. There are other garments in the closet for you to wear on special occasions. Girl, you know I love to shop, so you will have the opportunity to pick what you like, and to find something for Neeyla as well. Now hurry and get dressed for breakfast."

As I walked into the kitchen, I encountered Fatima, who was especially enthused while preparing breakfast. She was singing gospel songs and making melodies. Fatima's favorite thing to do in the world was to pour out her heart in the labor of her hands while preparing delicious meals. "Surprise, Tracy Lynn! I have prepared your favorite, pancakes, frying sausages, scrambled eggs, and rice. Yes, we also eat American food. Reena made certain of that many years ago. No fufu this morning."

Both Reena and Adebiyi laughed in unison with Fatima. Breakfast was equally delicious and tasty. Fatima's pancakes were golden brown and crunchy around the edges, and topped with generous servings of thick maple syrup. Breakfast was quieter than usual, with Reena and Adebiyi exchanging penetrating stares, with little dialogue.

"Well, it's time for me to examine eyes and put in a day's work." Adebiyi gently kissed Reena on her cheek, gave me a warm hug, and joined his waiting attendant.Afterwards, Reena and I fastidiously put on our matching iros and bubbas, topping them with the sunny geles.

Before long, Amir arrived, speaking in his usual heavily accented voice. "Good morning, everyone! Are we ready for the first day of school?"

Reena's eyes had become glowing brown marbles. "Hey there, driver." She chuckled. "We ready, and check out my beautiful little Yoruban princess."

"Wow! She is breathtaking!"

"Yes, she is," Reena declared.

I blushed and said, "Thanks, Amir."

We all headed out the gate along with Adawa,who was the gatekeeper,and drove to the far end of Mid-town, passing a colorful parade of vendors and sulky looking buildings with corrugated metal roofs and mismatched boards. My attention shifted between Adawa's detachment and Reena and Amir's banter. Suddenly, I thought, *Aunt Reena sure is enjoying Amir's company.* They were joking and cajoling way more than she and Adebiyi ever did. *I'm just saying. Hmph, if you ask me, I would say Aunt Reena act like she is still going—going to do it with somebody.* I decided not to pass judgment on my sweet aunt, and just kept on staring out the window rather than dealing with Adawa's penetrating stares, wondering if he was psycho.

Along the way, we encountered countless men and women who were also wearing similar clothes in bold and bright hues.

"Aunt Reena, what are the men's clothes called?" I questioned.

Before she could answer, Adawa broke his silence and said, "The hat is called a fila; the trousers are called sokotos; and the shirt is called a gbariye. However, the buba is a shirt for both men and women."

Taken by his words, I watched Adawa for a minute, because this was as much as I had ever heard him say. I still thought he was a strange fellow. Adawa then told me that he was studying fashion design as a minor, and accounting as a major, at the University of Lagos, and was working for the Olujares to help support himself. Adawa was very tall, gaunt, with handsome native features and a thinly manicured moustache. I often caught him watching me when he thought I wasn't looking.

"Here we are, my dears, and truly enjoy your classes. I am going to pick up some tourist from the airport today and check on Adaeze. She is getting bigger each day, for soon, the twins will be here. I should be back an hour or so earlier before your session ends."

"See you then, and thanks, Amir," said Reena.

CHAPTER 22

# LITTLE LAGOS PREPARATORY SCHOOL

The Little Lagos Preparatory School for Girls, a newly built facility that had been in operation for over twenty years, taught general education courses to girls between the ages of five and twelve.

After that, they would enroll in high school. A procession of cars was filing into the teacher's parking lot as we walked into the double wide doors of the building. Inside, the walls were teeming with posters boasting quotes and Little Lagos flyers. At the rear entry, next to the main office was a quote in fancy gold letters against a bright pink background that read In Training to Wear My Crown.

A young woman, who appeared to be in her twenties, arose from her seat and greeted us. "Welcome back, Dr. Olujare! I see you brought Tracy with you."

"Yes, this is Tracy. She will be teaching with me this summer."

"Welcome to Little Lagos, Tracy. I'm Uche."

Uche was wearing bright orange stilettos and matching accessories, with a multicolored, tight-fitting dashiki dress. She was also wearing her hair in a tight up-do of box braids. "Dr. Olujare, allow me to walk you to your room. Maintenance has been painting all summer, so everything is fresh like new. Don't worry, all your things are placed back exactly as you left them. I made certain of that."

We walked down a long corridor of classrooms all containing the same wooden desks, with storage on the top of each desk. To my surprise, Adawa walked up and gave Uche the biggest hug out of nowhere. I stood in awe for a moment, because I was still wondering if Adawa actually talked, let alone hug on somebody.. Oh, he could talk all right. As we were walking down the hall, they began jeering and hi-fiving each other. I soon discovered that they were both college students at Lagos State when Adawa declared, "Hey, we will soon be graduating seniors, and done with the maddening advanced mathematics, advanced calculus, and accounting classes. No more Mr. Yogi Beary mathematics to rob of us sleep again."

They teasingly joked of their professor.

"Adawa, Dr. Olujare informed me that Tracy is also an English major. Well, Dr. Olujare definitely takes pride in her profession, and perhaps is creating countless future English majors by her mere presence here. Well, at least she is not to be compared with Mr. Yogi Beary, our accounting professor. He is equally mean and vicious." They laughed.

Aunt Reena's room was a colorful display of anchor charts, with countless golden honey bees anchored around the room. All of the crates and storage bins were all also in lively shades of golden yellow.

Posted across the top of her chalkboard was Madame CJ Walker's quote, "Don't sit down and wait for the opportunities to come; get up and make them." There, in the midst of the Motherland, Reena was celebrating a self-proclaimed African American millionaire, who, from distant shores, had consulted the Motherland for her medicinal herbs for hair growth and stimulation. In doing so, Madame CJ had given her life to teaching others how to adjust their crowns. There were multi-volumes of books, dictionaries, and encyclopedias sitting on immaculate shelves.

"Aunt Reena, your classroom is so reflective of your personality. It's so sunny and cheerful, and I love the honey bee theme."

"Bees are symbolic of industry and work ethics, which I try to instill in my students. They must not only be taught the books, but the true character of success," remarked Reena.

Meanwhile, Adawa and Uche hung out in the hallway while intermittently poking their heads into the classroom. Reena walked quietly to her desk, where I saw a nameplate embossed in bright gold letters and the inscription Dr. Reena Olujare. She then handed me an agenda, which she instructed me was routine procedure for the children as they entered the room each day.

"We begin each day with our morning prayer after the students have placed their book bags in their desk. Afterwards, we recite our national pledge of allegiance, including our student pledge. They will then remove the language books from the bottom of the desk and complete the language warm-up, which will be placed on the chalkboard at the end of each day. After completion, you will volunteer the students to orally give the correct response for each of the warm-up exercises. After they are done with the warm-up, you will introduce the lesson for the day by guiding them through it with a mini-lesson. Also, intrigue them with the learning objective by posing an anticipatory set question. That way, you will engage all of your pupils. At times, you may open the story for them by allowing them to read it with you. However, you will primarily time their reading to build reading stamina and fluency. Additionally, you will learn to converse in the old language of Yoruba with the students as part of the language practice each day. I know that this sounds like a lot; however, no worries here. You will assist me for the first week by monitoring our students and grading papers. Are you still excited?"

"Yes, but a little nervous."

"Don't be. They are all children. In fact, we have fifth grade, and you will love them."Uche stepped back into the room, smiling casually, and said, "Dr. Olujare, you have a few minutes left before the general assembly with our parents begins."

"I will be right there. Okay, Miss Tracy, let's go and meet out students' parents."

The auditorium was a bright canvas of teachers, students, and parents. Some wore traditional attire, yet others resembled a more Westernized look. Reena gracefully led us down the front row seats while I pranced quietly behind her. The school's superintendent of education, along with the founder, was standing at the podium. The founder was a short, broad-shouldered woman, heavy voiced woman. . She was also wearing a buba, iro, and gele, only she had a sash wrapped around hers. I'd forgotten what the sash was called.

"Greetings, parents, students, teachers, and support staff. We are certainly glad that you have chosen to dedicate a portion of your child's summer to educational pursuit and higher learning. Little Lagos Training School for Girls was founded with only ten members in its inception. Now, by God's grace, we are a thousand-plus strong students who are gaining an edge on their peers through preparatory courses and socialization skills. The Bibles says to train up a child in the way that he should go, and when he is old, he will not depart from it. Ladies and gentlemen, as we know, learning initially begins at home, and then is transferred to school. I am honored to have your presence at our illustrious school for girls, because as the sign in the lobby states, 'We are training future queens to wear their crowns.' We are training our girls not only on the fundamentals, but also how to walk in destiny. I will not bore you with a long speech this afternoon, because I'm a firm believer that actions speak louder than words. After a brief message from our superintendent, you will be directed to your child's homeroom teacher. We pray that Little Lagos proves to be a learning experience for both parents and child. Lastly, we will end our summer session at the end of July with an arts and crafts festival, which the children will conduct. Thank you, and may God richly bless each and every one of you. Mr. Superintendent, you may now address your audience.""Thank you again, but I believe my wife has said it all. Please be dismissed to your child's homeroom teacher."

After the meeting, the parents trickled in and out of the room as Reena greeted them in both Yorubi and English. "E-Karsun [good afternoon]," said Reena in articulate tones. A friendly family dressed in native attire entered the classroom, greeting both Reena and me. "E-Karsun, Reverend and Mrs. Adesola. I see that you are bringing Afolomi to us."

"Yes, she has been very excited about coming here early and bright on Monday morning."

"Well, that's the spirit," remarked Reena. "Reverend and Mrs. Adesola, this is my assistant, Tracy Lynn."

"Pleased to meet you, Tracy Lynn. We are the Adesolas, Reena's pastors. Afolomi is our youngest child."

"It is my pleasure," I said.

"Reena has told us so much about you, and you are even more precious in person."After all the parents and students had made their grand entrances, Reena, Adawa, and Uche decided to give me a tour of the entire building. We traversed the classrooms, cafeteria, and playground. As we sat in the afternoon sun, before long, we saw Amir driving quickly towards the front of the building, and knew it was time to go. Adawa decided to stay back so that he could assist the superintendent with the locking of the building, but something told me there was more to it than met the eye. They looked more like boyfriend and girlfriend to me."Thanks again, and nice meeting you, Uche," I said as I headed back to the classroom."Tracy Lynn, would you like to go with us to the movies on Saturday?"

"Yes, this sounds good, and I would love to go."

As I walked quietly up the hall, Amir had already joined Reena back in the classroom. Wwhat I witnessed next would be the shock of my life, and would trigger a succession of future climatic events that I would rather choose to soon forget. My sweet Aunt Reena was kissing and hugging Amir in a loving embrace. I backed away very quietly so as not to be seen. Amir told Reena that everything would be all right, and hugged her tightly. Wild thoughts of Aunt Reena in an adulterous affair with Amir flooded my brain. Aunt Reeena was going to get herself in world of trouble, and if Adebiyi found out, he was going to kill her. Hearing Amir's footsteps walking back into the hallway, I darted quickly into one of the adjoining empty classrooms so as not to be seen by Amir. Things were starting to get a little fiery on the horizon.

That night, I heard Uncle Adebiyi and Aunt Reena yelling in the night, and later I heard Aunt Reena crying. "Reena I'm warning you that if you do not stop seeing him, you will be sorry. Trust me! I promise you that you will pay for it!" shouted Adebeyi. I had never heard him speak this way before, so it made me sad. Suddenly, I felt connected to a distant past that I wanted to entirely forget. Miquel and Neeyla had fought so much over finances and Miquel's cheating. Therefore, I was no stranger to arguments, but I couldn't even imagine Aunt Reeena and Uncle Adebiyi arguing. To me, they had always seemed like the perfect couple. On top of that, I couldn't wrap my mind around my sweet aunt liking another man. Big Momma had always called her "hot in the pants," but I never saw it that way. Besides that, perhaps Amir was merely consoling her, since she and Adebiyi were obviously at odds. However, from what Amir was saying, it seems he knew about Reena and Amir.

CHAPTER 23

# LAGOS MARKET DAY

Saturday morning aroused within me great curiosities of commotion and noise throughout the house.

Wandering into the kitchen, I found Fatima accompanied by a short, squat, tight-fisted woman.

"Good morning," I said.

"Good morning, Tracy Lynn! This is Lotus, our housekeeper." She turned and smiled at me, saying, "Ekaro," which I gathered meant "good morning." Fatima had forewarned me to be sure to keep things I wanted off the floor because Lotus would sweep them up in a wild rage into the trash. After acknowledging me, and staring me up and down, she continued to pull all of the pots and pans out of the cabinets, telling Fatima that the kitchen was totally unorganized and a hot mess. I could tell from that first encounter that Lotus was actually the one who was the hot mess, standing there, pulling all of those dishes out of that cabinet like that, with Fatima just standing there, letting her do it. After all, Fatima loved that kitchen.

Before long, Reena and Adebiyi came strolling through the kitchen. Fatima told them that breakfast was waiting outside on the patio, and for me to join them. Breakfast was an abundance of fried plantains, omelet soufflé, and pickled okra. Both Reena and Adebiyi were cordial, and wearing looks of exasperation on their faces.

"Did you sleep well? And do you like the morning's breakfast?" Aunt Reena asked."It's great," I said. "Fatima is so talented."

"Yes, she is," they both said.

"Aunt Reena and Uncle Adebiyi, do you suppose that I could go to the movies with Uche and Adawa this evening?"

"Why, certainly. That would be just great. We want you to experience all phases of our Nigerian culture here, and not just part of it."

"I didn't think Adawa even talked until I saw him engaging with Uche. Boy, he can talk all right." I laughed.

"Well, this just means that since he opened up to you, you are indeed his friend. Honey, go on out there and have a good time with your friends," Reena intoned.

Without notice, Lotus just burst right through the back door and pounced down, breathing heavily at the table, making herself a home. She helped herself to a hearty serving of plantains, omelets, and pickled okra. Between spitty mouthfuls, she said, "Mr. Olujare, I have been working for you how long?"

"Well, I imagine for as long as Reena and I have been married, a little more than fifteen years."

"Aye," said Lotus between more mouthfuls of soufflé. Fatima informed me that she'd received a raise this summer.

"Lotus, Lotus, you have a misunderstanding here."

"Yeah, Mr. Olujare."

"I didn't exactly give Fatima a raise. I merely gave her a stipend for taking care of things while I'm away in the States."

"If you ask me, I think Fatima needs to take housekeeping 101. I leave for a few weeks, and this place is an absolute wreck. The kitchen is in an uproar, and Reena, it's dusty as all outdoors in there."

"Lotus, darling, did you take your medication? I am worried about you," questioned Fatima.

"Well, you need to worry about getting all of that dust out of this house, with your lazy self. I bet you can't find a speck of dust on that garden back there."

Aunt Reena started laughing real loudly, and Adebiyi smiled and just shook his head, winking at Reena. All the while, I could see his hands rubbing her backside. I was just glad they had made up.

"Tracy Lynn, you will become accustomed to Lotus and Fatima. They have been best friends since grade school. Sometimes they will argue until the crack of dawn, but both are inseparable friends. We just let them go at it, because they will never stop. If it's not about cleaning the house, or which songs to sing at church, then it's about the color of lipstick. But those two—I don't know what we would do without them, because they certainly keep things in perspective around here."

Lotus looked at Reena and said, "Reena, wouldn't you agree that Fatima spends all of her time in that garden, and polishing her lips and nails? It is not like she is going to get a man anytime soon, because all the young men are already taken. I mean, look at her. She is practically senior citizen, nursing home material. She couldn't get a man if she wanted to."Fatima just smiled and said, "I suppose you can."

We laughed again, but Lotus didn't think it was so funny. "Young lady, what's your name again?" Lotus asked me.

I smiled and said, "Tracy Lynn."

"Miss Tracy, when I was your age, I had them turning their heads left and right. Fatima knows the deal. We got into a fist fight over one boy when we were in the seventh grade because he decided that he liked me better."

"Lotus, there you go, reliving the prehistoric times."

"Fatima, let's go to the market today."

"Now you're talking. Sweet egusi soup is calling my name."

Fatima decided to enhance the mood by playing some upbeat African drum instrumentals and Reena, Fatima, and I, along with Lotus, all pitched in to give the house a general cleaning. After placing all the pots and pans back in the cabinets to Lotus's liking, Aunt Reena and I decided to clean the baths, since washing dishes was one of my least favorite things to do. Fatima took it upon herself to mop all of the floors, both upstairs and downstairs, while Lotus dusted and freshened the entire house thoroughly. Afterwards, we all piled into the car for an afternoon trip to downtown Lagos.

Market that day was sprawling in a sea of color. We advanced the market like young children going to the carnival for the first time. Aunt Reena, I'm certain, was accustomed to it, along with the others, but for me, it was my fondest wish come true. Brightly colored tents dotted the horizon as vats overflowed with fresh produce, tomatoes, and habanero peppers in bright reds that glistened in the afternoon sun. Vendors of all shapes and sizes displayed a colorful food fiesta of mouthwatering, delectable goods. It was like a giant grocery store, only outside, and that made it even more intriguing. As we neared one hot food vendor, the smell of sugar and cinnamon hung heavily in the air, creating an intoxicating aroma that reminded me of Grandma Carrie's kitchen. Golden brown puff puffs bobbed in hot oil until they turned a deep golden.

"Puff puffs!" shouted Aunt Reena. "You absolutely have to taste this one. They are like Africa's Shirley's Donuts."

The vendor filled four small plastic bags full of the sweet brown puff puffs for all. "Today I give you a discount of three hundred naira."

Aunt Reena eagerly paid him, and handed the puff puffs to us. I quickly popped one in my mouth. They were sweet and crunchy on the outside, and real soft on the inside. I was hooked for life.

"You like them?" asked Fatima.

"You bet," I said, while stuffing my waiting lips.

The sights and sounds of the market awakened within my spirit a deep belongingness within. Plentiful heaps of groundnuts, which we call peanuts, were doled out in pintfuls to waiting customers. Mounds of bitter greens, fresh okra, stockfish, and crayfish were in abundance throughout the market. As we made our way through the market, both Lotus and Fatima filled their shopping bags with goods sufficient for the week by bargaining with select vendors until they reached an agreement on price. Meanwhile, Reena and I stumbled upon a colorful display of Ankara tops and dresses. I selected two in bright red and deep green.

After a while, we met up with the others and decided to take a break at another hot food vendor, where Fatima said that we would be having dinner. By that time, the sun was sweltering hot, and I must have been dripping sweat buckets. The waiter greeted us and offered cool glasses of water, which we all quickly drank.

A smiling woman, who was arrayed in a colorfulbuba and gele, greeted us in English with the signature Nigerian accent. "Good afternoon, Dr. Olujare, Fatima, and Lotus! What would you like today?"

"Good afternoon, Ada! We will be having the egusi soup special."

The smiling woman wrote down our order, and gave it to the women in the back. As we sat down and waited for our order, Lotus and Fatima had a short run in about the food that was ordered.

"Fatima, you always order the same thing over and over, and besides, how do you know that this young lady will like egusi soup?"

"Ladies, calm down! We are in public!" Reena spoke hotly.

Shortly, the waiter brought out a large bowl of spicy soup, pounded yam, golden brown akara, and cool limeade drinks. We just sat there for about an hour, sipping soup and watching the parade of marketers as they strolled by. Some were carrying their wares on their heads, while others sold from cramped places.

"Fatima, what is egusi soup?" I questioned.

"It consists of egusi, which are crushed melon seeds, onions, peppers, crayfish, stockfish, palm oil, and spinach. You see, girl, these ingredients will keep your skin looking healthy with a nice youthful glow, and when you are my age, you will be looking young, like me, your Auntie Fatima."

Lotus shook her head and said, "When hell freezes over."

"Mind your business, Lotus."

"Also, pounded yam is made essentially the same way as mashed potatoes. After the yams are boiled and mashed, they are turned over and over with a large spoon on heat until they resemble the consistency of fufu."

"I think I actually like the taste of fufu now."

"Before you go back home, I will show you how to make the akara cakes for Sunday dinner. They are seasoned black-eyed peas that are liquefied and fried with peppers, onions, and spices."

"Ohh, my grandmother in Mississippi cooks black-eyed peas on New Year's for good luck."

"Does she really?" Lotus inquired with a wild look of fascination in her eyes. If you'd asked me, I would have sworn that Lotus was a black magic woman.

Evening carried us back to our car, with Lotus behind the wheel because she said Fatima drove way too slow for her liking. We sped past vendors dipping in and out of traffic at record speeds. My heart felt like it was at the bottom of my feet. I said a little prayer to myself, thinking all the while, *Lord, please don't let this crazy woman kill us all.* We must have hit every rut and pothole along the way before we finally swerved full speed ahead in the driveway. We all hit the brakes at the same time, because we thought we would go through the window.

"Now *that's* good driving," she declared as she let out a deep sigh of relief. Was she practicing or what?

We all got out of the car in one big, mad, out-of-breath heap.

Aunt Reena asked, "Lotus, have you lost your damn mind, driving that fast?"

Lotus just pretended she didn't hear her, and filed right behind Fatima into the kitchen to put the groceries away. Reena shook her head and walked rapidly down the hall with me, and turned into her bedroom.

She had scarcely closed her door when I overheard her conversation on the telephone. I heard her telling someone, "I love Lotus to the core, and she has been with us forever, but I don't know about her shrewd temperament at times. It drives me crazy. If she doesn't stop it, she is going to boot herself out of a job. Just the other day, she came in and decimated the kitchen by pulling all of the pans from under the sink, saying the house was a wreck. I mean, she does good work, but Amir, I thought she would kill us all today. She was driving like a maniac. What's wrong with her?"

"Baby," I could hear him say. Oh my goodness, it was just like I thought it was. She was fooling around with that man, and he was her driver. *Where do they do that?* I wondered. I continued to eavesdrop, listening outside the door.

"Baby, listen. Don't worry about that. Find some reason to leave the house later so that I can hug and kiss away all of your worries. Besides, Lotus is just becoming erratic, and that comes with aging. Maybe you should encourage her to eat better and exercise. Good health does help fight dementia."

Oh, I was not witnessing this. Poor Adebiyi would be crushed. I closed my door quickly as I heard her walking back towards her door. Whatever Aunt Reena had going on, I did not want any part of it.

Deciding that I'd had enough, I jumped quickly up on the bed and decided to call Neelya.

"Hey, Ma! What you been doing?" I asked. For a moment, there was nothing but silence, and I intuitively knew that Neelya was in one of her moods.

Finally, Neeyla, very dryly, said, "It took you long enough to call. I could have been dead by now."

"Oh, honestly, Momma, I've been very busy with Aunt Reena and Fatima, so I called you the first chance I got." No amount of explaining was going to get to Neeyla when she was in one of those crazy moods. "Okay, Momma, I just called to say I love you, and will call you back tomorrow."

She had already hung up the phone before I could say good bye. *Oh well, I am used to it. I'll just beg her back tomorrow, and she will be fine after she's done pouting.* I quickly regathered my thoughts and contemplated what I would wear to the movies with Uche and Adawa. It was a little after five o'clock, and our movie date was at seven. I decided to wear my new bright red Ankara top, a denim skirt, and some Moroccan sandals. After a steamy hot bath and some fresh makeup, I decided to join the adults, who had gathered in the family room to watch a movie of their own.

Fatima was sprawled across the couch from Lotus, who appeared to be quiet this time and preoccupied with knitting. Reena and Adebiyi sat together in a roomy armchair. Just looking at the two of them would have made one think they were the happiest couple in the world, but I knew better, and looked away. They were watching a movie about a poor Nigerian girl who had later married a millionaire.

Lotus then looked circumspectly at me, and asked, "Girl, where are you going in that short skirt?"

"Actually, it's not that short, Lotus," I said.

"Oh yeah, girl, it is."

"Lotus, didn't I tell you to mind your business?" said Fatima.

"I'm going to the movies tonight with Uche and Adawa."

"Jesus, that college girl is hotter than a firecracker. Her entire business is walking around in dresses on that are two sizes too small for her and her backside, with Adawa literally worshipping her. I see that she is already rubbing off on you too."

"Lotus, why don't you just carry yourself to bed with all of this nonsense that no one wishes to hear. We've all had enough of it."

Reena managed to lighten the mood by saying, "Tracy Lynn, go on out there and have a good time with your friends."

Adawa's familiar knock sent me reeling to my feet, as I was eager to breathe some fresh air. Outside, Uche was waiting in a red convertible Camaro.

Adawa smiled and said, "Hello. Are you ready?"

"Without a doubt." I blushed.

"Then we are on our way," he said.

I skipped to the car, beaming with excitement. I very gently opened that candy apple red door and sat in the backseat, while Adawa sat in the front seat.

"Hey, Uche," I said. "Your car looks like something out of the movies. This car is so fantastic. By the way, you look nice too," I said.

"And so do you, Tracy," she said. "My father bought it for me and said that I can keep it as long as I keep my grades up."

"Girl, what kind of work does your father do for you to be riding like this?"

"He is a movie producer, and when I'm done with my schooling, I plan to work as his personal accountant."

"Tracy, Uche doesn't really have to work, but she likes to help her auntie, her father's sister, at the school," said Adawa.

"So you are related to the superintendents too. Girl, you really have it going on!"

"Well, trust me, none of my family members were born with it. It comes from a lot of hard work and steadfast prayer. I watched my father and mother pray, pray nonstop. It is our only hope."

"This is so true, Uche. Prayer has certainly helped me overcome some of the difficulties of my childhood."

"Anyway, I'm glad that you like the car, but I usually still drive my old car to work. That car and I go back to when my family was getting by. It is like an old companion that you never grow tired of."

"Yes, I know, right? Neeyla's car is old as well, and she calls it her 'Bessie.' Tell me, Uche, where are we heading?"

"We are going to downtown, to the outskirts of town known as Idumota, where the afrobeats make you want to shake, shake your booty to the music. Here you will experience music and night life like no other. It is also one of the biggest markets in Western Nigeria. You will see a lot of vendors still out there. What time is your curfew? Don't worry. We will have you back before midnight."

Uche then turned the music up and started singing and moving in place to the beat. It was a stirring mixture of African drum hip-hop that I had never heard before, but I liked it. Adwawa pulled a bottle of wine from under the seat, and poured a little in all of the cups, then offered me a cup as well.

"No, thanks. I don't drink," I said.

"Come on, lighten up. You have to learn to relax and let your hair down. It's actually a very mild drink. Come on, try it."

"All right, I'll try it," I said, deciding to take a small sip of the alcohol.

The taste reminded me of sweet, tangy cherries. The more I sipped the bright red liquor, the more it made me feel real warm deep down on the inside of my stomach. Suddenly, the tunes of the radio were turning and revolving around in my head, and I felt like I was floating. After driving through a dimly lit section of town, we rode past a group of college students who were waiting in a single-file line for movie tickets. Girls in short dresses, with heavy cleavage, stood wrapped tightly and juxtaposed against lustful lovers. After standing in line for a little while, Adawa and Uche caught up with some of their college friends.

"Ekarle [good evening] to you, Adawa and Uche," said the others.

"Hey now, and good evening to you too," they replied. "How are you guys?"

"This is our new friend from America, Tracy Lynn."

"Wow! What a bombshell," said one of the tall guys. "My name is Salathiel, and these are my friends, Carmine and Joseph."

"Pleased to meet you," said the others.

"Likewise," I said.

After some friendly conversation with the others, we finally made our way inside. The theater had identical rows of velvet-lined cushiony chairs, with heavy black velvet curtains draped around the entire circumference, giving it the appearance of an amphitheater. Eager patrons bearing bags of gugaru and epa, spicy popcorn and peanuts, soon crowded the theater until there were no more seats left. We sat in the middle rear section, and I decided to sit on the outside. Uche and Adawa sat together so that they could whisper to each other and tongue kiss during the entire movie. Salathiel decided to sit next to me, and I could feel him watching me the entire time, so I decided to say something to him. Salathiel was very fair-skinned and tall, with a deep Nigerian accent.

"Salathiel, you look different from the others."

He laughed and said, "Are you trying to tell me that I'm not dark enough to be an African?"

"No, you said that."

"Well, that is what you are implying. Admit it." He laughed. "It is because, Miss Tracy, my mother is English, and my father is Nigerian. So do you like the movie all right?""Well, it's okay, but I'm generally not a fan of blood and gore," I said. The movie was about a bitter feud between old friends that ended in bloodshed.

He laughed and said, "Typically, you women like movies with fairy tale endings, but in life, we must also accept not-so-happy endings."

After listening to his last remark, I decided that maybe I was talking too much to Salathiel, since I had only just met him.

CHAPTER 24

# CHURCH OF THE ROCK

Saturday night disappeared in a whirl, and turned into Sunday morning service at the Church of the Rock.

A colorful, bedazzled choir stood in adulation at the coming of the Lord. The entire sanctuary was filled with praise and worship. The mighty choir sang out loud as people were crying and dancing in the aisles. Some were speaking English, and others were speaking in their native tongues. Two faces that I had seen before were mounted on the platform of the pulpit. I soon realized that it was Aunt Reena's pastors, the Adesolas. Both were wearing white clergy attire, and momentarily, Lady Adesola began to render the most angelic version of "Sweet Holy Spirit" that I had ever heard before. The woman's voice sounded like an angel's, and the tears began to flow from my eyes, just as they were flowing from Aunt Reena's. All the while, Adebiyi held her in a loving embrace.

The pastor preached, "Though your sins be as scarlet, Jesus wants to make you whiter than snow."

I was thinking that Aunt Reena must be in her feelings, since she had been booed up with Amir. Distracted by many sights and sounds that reminded me of my own church, I could not help but notice that Salathiel and his family were standing directly across from us. One quick glance at his penetrating stare brought a flush of embarrassment to my cheeks. I imagined that he must have been staring at me the entire time, long before I saw him. I quickly surmised that the tall white woman who was standing next to him must have been his mom. She was just as tall, and had the same penetrating stare in her eyes. A short, broad-shouldered man was standing on the other side of her, holding a very small child with droopy cheeks and two curly ponytails. I guessed that it was his baby sister, because she looked just like them too.

When Salathiel realized that I was looking at them, he lit up like a Christmas tree, and just kept on smiling and waving at me every time I looked that way. After staring over at him a couple of times, I felt a sweet sensation going through my bones. Suddenly, I found myself crushing on a boy while I was standing right there in the house of the Lord. What a shame before God, when I should have been concentrating on what the preacher was saying, and not thinking about the opposite sex.

After the alter call, service ended with a benediction by the pastor. As we prepared to leave, Salathiel and his entire family approached us with warm and friendly smiles. "Tracy Lynn, these are my parents and baby sister."

"Hello," they all said in the most British-sounding accent that took me by surprise."Hello. I'm pleased to meet you," I told them.

"The same to you, and enjoy your stay in Nigeria," they said, as they turned to greet the pastor.

Salathiel traced my footsteps, and once we made it outside, he asked if he could see me again. Looking up at him just made my heart melt. I still had never kissed a boy before. I managed a very shy "Maybe."

This time, we had all traveled in separate cars that morning, so when we made it back, Fatima and Lotus were already putting the finishing touches on Sunday dinner. Afterwards, we all gathered in the dining room and ate a delicious meal fit for a king.

CHAPTER 25

# KEHINDE AND TAIWO'S NAMING CEREMONY

Early Monday morning greeted us with the sights and sounds of the workday ahead.

Monday morning carried us back to Little Lagos, with Amir's smiling face and joyful heart behind the wheel. Aunt Reena was beside herself, grinning. Everything that Amir said just made her giggle out loud like a school girl. There was no denying it; she was in love, but not with the right person. I prepared my heart for what was ahead. After breakfast, the girls were all lined up outside of the door as they waited to be seated in their assigned seats. After the tardy bell, Aunt Reena—well, for formal purposes, Dr. Olujare—and I both walked into the classroom to greet the students.

"Ekaro, and welcome to Little Lagos. I am Dr. Olujare, and this is my assistant, Mrs. Sandifer. I want you to know that your education is the greatest thing that you can ever own in your lifetime. We are here to ensure that you maximize all of your God-given potential." She then related to the students how she had worked as a maid in America while earning her college degree. "I was born Reena Mariella Sandifer in a small town called Money, Mississippi, where the cotton grows far beyond the winding dirt roads. My grandparents, Uncle Sammy and Big Momma, raised me, and did the best they could with what little they had, and today, I'm grateful."

June echoed Dr. Olujare's varied tales of faraway places and enchanted lands, which made the children's eyes glow in bewilderment. The days spun like the threads in an ancient spindle, and I became rehearsed in the language and customs of the Yoruba. The July heat was unbearably scorching hot, and the flies were building dunes in the sand. In the evening, the mighty Osun River paid homage to the ancients, and labor pains caused Adaeze to scream in the night, for inside her womb, the twins had begun conversing on their journey to the new world. The swift ax of the carpenter fell into the mighty river, and Kehinde, the elder twin, told Taiwo, the firstborn, that it was time to meet Amir and Adaeze.

At daybreak, Adeaze let out a deafening cry as the village mid-wife was in attendance. The elder brother Kehinde gave Taiwo a swift kick, and the first cry of the infant resounded in the morning air. Amir let out thunderous praise as the mid-wife handed his first-born son Taiwo over to him. As the tears welled in his eyes, Kehinde's head poked far out of Adaeze's womb. With a sharp cry from Adaeze, Kehinde's loud wail permeated the atmosphere, and the mighty Osun flowed in its banks. Both twins had made their journey into the new world. Both babies were simultaneously cleaned by the mid-wives and laid upon Adaeze's waiting bosom. Momentarily, Amir had begun singing and chanting songs of adulations and praise the entire time, while Adeaze silently wept with tears of joy over the birth of her sons. She kissed their inquisitive cheeks, and saw Amir's stature in Kehinde, and his soul in Taiwo. Her spirit was reflected in their glistening eyes. Meanwhile, the news of Amir's twins traveled in circles around Lagos and the village. Amir was the son of traders and textile weavers. He also had a small thriving business on the side, in addition to his daily runs as an airport driver, where he'd first become acquainted with the Olujares. He was known by many. This was Sunday, and the naming ceremony would be held on the following Saturday.

Meanwhile, Reena's cheeks glowed, and Fatima and Lotus argued over whether the twins should have traditional names.

"I think that there are so many twins with those names," remarked Lotus. "Reena, don't you think they should name them Amir Junior, like they do in your country?"

"Actually, Lotus, I think tradition means everything, since both twins can't be called Amir."

"Yeah, they can be named Amir I and Amir II," she said.

"Lotus, each child should be named in accordance with personality." Reena laughed.Momentarily, the phone began ringing off its hook, and Fatima answered. "Ekaro, this is the Olujare residence."

"Hello, Fatima, this is Amir. Please inform Reena and Adebiyi that my twins are born.""Yes, we heard. Good news travels fast."

"Oh, you already know about it! Wow, this is great! Please inform them that the naming ceremony will be the following Saturday at high noon."

"Amir, this is wonderful news. I'm so excited for you. How are Adaeze and the twins?"

"She is resting, and beside herself with excitement, and the girls cannot wait to dress and feed them! They are both very healthy, and handsome like their papa."

"Amir, you are a piece of work, but I couldn't be any happier for you, my kinsman. Well, we shall all see you Saturday, bright and early. Talk with you soon, and I will let Reena and the others know. Goodbye now."

Fatima informed the others, and she and Lotus began deciding on the food they would take to the ceremony. Meanwhile, Adaeze's mother sought the village priest for the naming of the twins.

The sun walked from behind the gray mountains and cast a splendid glare on the town. Both babies glowed in the favor of their father. The sun stood high on its ancient bluff, and smiled on the inhabitants. Saturday morning had arrived with the swiftness of cats' feet, and the town's elders, clothed in white, walked out of sleepy villages and traversed the terrain. The Church of the Rock was the community church on the outskirts of town in a quaint village where Amir and his kinsmen had been trading textiles for centuries. Shortly, a procession of people, attired in rich purples, royal blues, and sparkling golds, dotted the fiery horizon in one mass assemblage to the ceremony. Inside the walls of the church, a chorale of dancers were singing songs of worship and praise, thanking God for the blessing of the twins. The women wore royal blue with satin royal geles. All the elders, along with the paternal and maternal parents, were seated at the head of the church. The twins had been born seven days before to Amir and Adaeze Ibidun. "Ibidun" means "childbirth is sweet."

Prayer came down in the sanctuary as the mighty rains descending from Heaven. The attending priest and his attendants made supplications on behalf of Kehinde and Taiwo. The mighty priest declared, "Kehinde will lead his people and bridge commerce between the nations. He, from an early age, will embrace the gift of his ancestors, and will study what is written in the books concerning commerce and trade. His trademark will be established upon the four corners of the earth. He will walk in the ways of leadership and problem solving. He shall be his family's fortune. Whereas, Taiwo will, from an early age, embrace equity and fairness. He, too, will study in the books concerning equanimity and the laws of the land. He shall serve as a voice to those who have no voice. He will set at liberty those who have been bruised by circumstance outside of their control. He shall be a great ruler of his people.

"Therefore, we give water so that the twins will know neither thirst nor enemies in this life; we give palm oil so that the twins shall transition into a smooth and easy life, filled with love and no friction. We give bitter kola nut so that the child will have a very long life. We give plain cola nut to repel the evils of life. We give honey for a happy and sweet life. We give pepper for a fruitful life with many children. We give dried fish so that the children will remain in their natural environment with the love of the parents and never be overcome, even in difficult times. We give salt so that the children's lives will not be ordinary, but filled with happiness and substance, causing them to preserve all good things. We give a pen so that the twins will not use the pen for evil, and it will not return likewise. And more importantly, we give the Holy Bible so that the twins may have the knowledge of God, and God will be with them as they follow God's paths."

Both Adaeze and Amir, who were wearing royal blue and bright gold, carried their twins as great decrees and proclamations were decreed over them. Afterwards, the crowd danced before them, bestowing great monetary gifts, while touching them to Adaeze's and Amir's bosoms for the future of their twins.

Service turned out, and the crowd shifted to Amir's home, which was a short distance from the church. Tables were filled with running-over servings of jolef rice, palm nut stew, greens, fufu, abacha, and ankara cakes, laid out for the arriving crowd. The mighty drums echoed throughout the village, singing the songs of their ancestors. Great dancers struck out mighty cords with the reverberating beats, paying homage to their Creator.

Salathiel and I walked a great distance from the music and dance, and locked our lips in the embrace of a first kiss, exchanging our heartbeats beats with those of the drums and subsequently, after many passionate kisses turned to burning lust, I would soon share my Mom's fate and ultimately have to kiss my scholarship to Rust College goodbye. Adaeze's golden gele dazzled in the afternoon sun as she smiled favorably upon her babies. She and Amir were now dancing in loving adulation before the crowd. Aunt Reena gazed from afar. Her countenance was repressed with uncertainty. She tucked her smile in the bottom of her purse, picked up her phone, and called Neeyla for consolation. Reena's eyes foretold that her heart was comtemplating the unimaginable, for she was caught in the middle of a three-way love affair.

## A TRIBUTE TO MY MOTHER

Mother, you took a little, and turned it into much.
You calmed my fears with the gentleness of your touch.
When I was little, and would fall down,
You taught me how to walk on higher ground.

You consoled my fears, and taught me faith through the years.

Moreover, you taught me right from wrong,
And always told me, "Trouble don't last long."
Yes, you showed me when I went astray,
That God does not want us to go that way.

Mother, you taught me grace, strength, and dignity,
And said that it was God's way for me.
When I was sick, you prayed for God's healing,For in the
midnight hour, you would always be kneeling.

You gladly took me to church on the Sabbath,
And proclaimed that serving God is more than a habit.
You taught me faith don't come by sight,
For Jesus works in the quiet of the night.

And when you put God first in all you do,
He will gladly repay it back to you.
So on this special day, we pay tribute for all the love you kindly giveth.

Yes, Mother, we honor you on this day, for you taught that Jesus is the only way.
Your love and kindness has been tried and true in all the sacrifices and things you do.

So, I proudly say, Neeyla Jean, I love you.